"Sister Maxine has had a wealth of teaching experience and has endeared herself to many children. Her suggestions to teachers are forthright, comfortably delivered, and readily applicable.

"The 'Teacher Info,' 'Did You Know,' and 'Helpful Hint' insets and will be especially welcomed by inexperienced teachers.

"Sister Maxine's suggestions are adaptable and stimulating. Catechists in Catholic schools and parish religion programs will find valuable approaches, information, and instructional procedures in this volume."

Sr. Francis Assisi, C.S.A.
Regional Director, Religious Education
Archdiocese of Mobile

"This is a unique collection of topics to challenge both teachers and students, and they will have 'fun' while making their faith come alive. Church feasts, saints' days, legal holidays, and celebrations they never heard of—'Popcorn Poppin' Month' and 'National Yo-Yo Day'—will bring smiles and laughter.

"Turn a page and you have a surprise, a refreshing way to help children make prayer a natural part of their lives. Sister Maxine's ideas will add spice to your lesson plans and will help your students to appreciate their faith more."

Sister Mary Denis Bruck, S.L.

100 *Fun Ways to* Livelier Lessons

MAXINE INKEL, S.L.

TWENTY-THIRD PUBLICATIONS
Mystic, Connecticut 06355

Twenty-Third Publications
185 Willow Street
P.O. Box 180
Mystic, CT 06355
(203) 536-2611
800-321-0411

ISBN 0-89622-654-9
Library of Congress Catalog Card Number 95-60421
Printed in the U.S.A.

Dedication

In loving memory of my parents,
Oliva Inkel and M. Anna Bouffard Inkel,
who gave me and my siblings,
Denis, Roland, Jill, Candide, Rolande, Maurice, and Joseph G.,
the kind of home that nurtured faith and talents.

Acknowledgments

Writing a book is like being at the end of a line of mountain climbers! Those ahead have prepared the way and share in large part the success of one's arriving at the summit!

I gratefully acknowledge those who helped me with this book:

•Sister Benigna (now Maurita) Hunt, RSM, who started me writing in Grade 7, half a century ago, and I've never stopped. That's a good teacher's influence for you!

•My congregation, the Sisters of Loretto, founded in 1812 to serve in the Church as teachers, and who have done so for almost 200 years!

•Sister Vincent Clare Hauptmann, S.L. (retired, in name only!) who has joyfully prayed her beads the livelong day for me while I put these activities together.

•Twenty-Third Publications, especially Gwen Costello, who, as my very capable editor, constantly reminded me of my goal: to help catechists spread the Good News through lively religion classes.

What more can I say? From up here the view is mighty fine!

Table of Contents

100 Fun Ways to Livelier Lessons

Introduction

You are a catechist! Great! This book is for you—especially for you!

Since, as the *Catechism of the Catholic Church* says, "Catechesis is an education in the faith...." (Prologue II, 5), I include in the term "catechist": parents, teachers, DREs, pastors, extended family members, and, yes, our bishops, too; in short, all of us who are in any way involved in trying to lead others to God.

In this book you will find 100 activities. That's right—ONE HUNDRED—different ways to help you keep children busy, interested, and happy during religion classes and to lead them joyfully to God.

Have you ever noted that when you have a happy experience, you tend to want to remember everything and everyone connected with it? On the other hand, you're more than glad to forget experiences that have bored you silly!

It's the same with the children we teach. If we present the great truths of our faith to children in lively ways that make them happy, they will more easily connect these truths with something good, to be remembered, treasured, and, hopefully, lived! So, what I've done in this book is to present 100 small, practical, and inexpensive (for the most part) ways to try to do this.

Ten Monthly Units

The activities are divided into ten monthly units, with ten activities for each month of the school year. But, they are very flexible, structured in such a way that you can adapt them to different dates, feasts, grade levels and, in many cases, for use at home with families. For example, though the activity for Francis of Assisi is in October, you can use it at any time of the year when you want to focus on "making mistakes"

(the theme of that particular activity).

As you thumb through the pages, you will notice that, although I used the Catholic calendar extensively, I also included national holidays, great persons, seasons of the year, and many other familiar and not-so-familiar occasions.

I have tried to adapt the activities to children in grades one through five, keeping in mind that they can't sit still long and that they can't listen for more than a few minutes at a time. Children like to move and they enjoy humor. I tried to include both. I also included ways to teach children to love, respect, and understand the poor, the powerless, the sick, and the elderly, thus introducing them early in life to selflessness and consideration of others—qualities so characteristic of Jesus.

Above all, these activities are aimed at helping children to develop a personal relationship with Jesus. They present Jesus to children as someone they can believe in, be friends with, imitate, and depend upon as they face the many problems that are part of growing up today. To keep them in touch with Jesus, every activity has a prayer component, one that you can use quickly and easily.

After you have used these simple activities for a while, my hope is that you will start developing your own, continually finding new ways to create livelier lessons. Then you will no doubt catch yourself saying: Behold the lilies of the field! See the birds of the air! Look at that pretty piece of glass! What an unusual rock! Suddenly all creation—all people, places, and things—will inspire you to share your joy with those you teach.

Sr. Maxine Finkel, S.L.

SEPTEMBER

SUN	MON	TUES	WED	THURS	FRI	SAT

Ideas & Activities

1. Labor Day
2. Mary's Birthday
3. Saint Peter Claver
4. Rosh Hashanah
5. Grandparent's Day
6. Yom Kippur
7. Triumph of the Cross
8. Our Lady of Sorrows
9. Sapphire Birthdays
10. Michaelmas Day

1 *Labor Day*

Walk back and forth across the room looking puzzled. When you have the full attention of the children, stop abruptly and ask: "Did God work?"

Expect all kinds of answers depending upon the children's concept of God as either near them and accessible or way out there in the great beyond.

Then go to the board and write: "Genesis 2:3—and on the seventh day, God rested." Ask: "What had God been doing that required rest?" Lead the children to the concept that God was obviously willing to be described by the sacred writers as a "working person" to teach us that work is good.

Tell the children that on Labor Day we celebrate good workers and good work. Invite them to take turns doing pantomimes of various kinds of work. You might want to list various jobs on slips of paper, including blue- and white-collar jobs and jobs in the home, for example, delivering mail, playing the violin, doing dishes, cutting wood, driving a truck, etc. After the class guesses each pantomime, invite children to stand and stretch out their arms in blessing and repeat this prayer after you: "Holy God, please bless all who work in (name the work), especially those in our families." Invite children to name specific persons who do that work, if applicable. Continue until all the types of work on your slips of paper have been pantomimed and prayed over.

Helpful Hint: Let me mention here that in order to be fair about giving every child a chance to participate (in this or any other activity), you should try the following. Make a set of hand-held cards on which the children's names are written—one child per card. You can then shuffle the cards and call on the child whose name lands on top. This keeps the children alert, since they don't know whose name is coming up!

I realized how important these cards were to my class one year when, just as I was about to pitch a beat-up set of them, the children leaped on them, wanting them to "play school with." I flipped a card to see which lucky child would take that year's beat-up cards home!

Children have a deep-seated sense of fairness, and I think they like these "take-turns" cards because the cards help keep their teacher fair.

2 Mary's Birthday

Teacher Info

Tell the children that Mary's birthday has been celebrated on September 8 since the seventh century—about thirteen hundred years ago!

Our Blessed Mother must certainly have had all kinds of celebrations down through the ages. But she will no doubt also love this one prepared by you and your class.

Give everyone a 2" x 4" piece of paper, any color. Have the children fold the paper in half to form a "box." Then, have them draw ribbons on it to make it look like a gift box.

After the gift boxes are ready, ask the children to think about what "gift" they could give Mary for her birthday. Suggest a few yourself and let the children suggest some. Examples might be: being attentive and cooperative in class on a day when you don't feel like it; being gracious to a classmate or teacher that you don't especially like; not pushing to be first in line; picking up litter; asking your mom or dad if you can help them; spending time with an elderly person (crabby or nice); saying prayers more carefully…and so forth.

After the "gifts" are decided upon (no need for them to say aloud what it is), have each of the children pretend that the gift is in their hand. Then have them slip the "gift" into the box, seal it with scotch tape, and write on it: "Happy Birthday, Mother Mary, from_____." Next, gather around a picture or statue of Mary and have each child deliver the "gift" while the class sings, "Happy Birthday" to Mary.

Helpful Hint

Always try to do class activities right along with the children. This brings you closer to them, and if there are problems with your project, you can adjust as you go.

Have you ever planned a project that you didn't try before class, only to find that it was impossible to do? It's happened to me. In a case like this, just stop and tell the children you made a mistake. Ask them to help you adjust the activity. Someone always comes up with the right solution!

❸ Saint Peter Claver

Teacher Info

For this activity, you will need to explain the following words:

Patron: a saint to whom one can pray to obtain special blessings from God. (You might want to have a list of these around. Don't tell anybody, but I get my lists from the medals section of religious goods catalogues. Honest—they're great!)

Mission: a place where the gospel is not yet known.

Missionary: a person who has a special calling from Jesus to go out and spread the Word of God.

You will also need a world map.

St. Peter Claver's feast day is September 9th. He was a missionary to black slaves in South America and the West Indies, and he has been declared the patron saint of Catholic missions among black people.

Introduce this activity by saying: "In the world, there are many places in which people do not yet know about or believe in Jesus (pause to let that sink in). Missionaries are people who go to such places to teach about Jesus and also to serve the needs of the people as Jesus might have done. Now let's all pretend that we are missionaries. Let's each choose a country that we would like to go to and share God's Word."

Invite the children to take turns going to the world map to choose a country where they would like to be "missionaries." If no one chooses the United States, you choose it. Alert the children to the fact that in our own country there are many people who do not believe in God or in Jesus; they, too, need to hear God's Word.

Ask children to think of ways that they can do missionary work right here in the classroom. Possible answers might be: praying for missionaries, supporting the missions, and asking God to call many persons to be missionaries.

At the end of this activity, invite children to stand and stretch a hand of blessing toward their chosen countries on the map, and have them repeat this prayer after you:

Holy God / Loving God / there are many people in these countries / who have not yet received your Word. / Please send missionaries to them. / We

promise to support your missionaries / with our prayers. / And, please, God, / call some of us in this class / to be missionaries someday / who will take your Word / to many countries. / We ask this in Jesus' name. Amen.

4 Rosh Hashanah

Teacher Info

The words Rosh Hashanah mean "beginning of the year." At this special time, people of the Jewish faith pray for three things: 1) God's forgiveness, 2) a good year, and 3) a long life.

During Rosh Hashanah, Jewish people say three special groups of prayers.

The first group reminds everyone that God is in charge. The second group reminds people that God hears their prayers and will help them in the current situations in their lives. The third group reminds people that God remembers their deeds.

During this holiday a special horn, called a shofar, is blown. The shofar is made from a ram's horn.

On the chalkboard, a poster, or a piece of newsprint, list these three things that our Jewish sisters and brothers pray for at Rosh Hashanah: 1) God's forgiveness, 2) a good year, and 3) a long life. Then ask the children if we pray for similar things in our Catholic faith. Answers might include the following:

As Catholics, we pray for forgiveness…

…at the Confiteor of the Mass,

…when we say an Act of Contrition,

…when we go to confession,

…when we say our night prayers.

As Catholics, we pray for a good year…

…at our own New Year celebrations,

…on birthdays.

As Catholics, we pray for a long life…

…on birthdays,

…at baptism,

…in the sacraments of marriage and anointing.

The point of this discussion is to show the great similarities between the Jewish and Catholic faiths, accenting likenesses rather than differences, and to help children develop respect for people of other faiths. Conclude by gathering around your prayer table as three children offer these petitions (light a candle before you begin):

Reader One: Great God of all, we ask for forgiveness now and every day.

Reader Two: Let this be a good year for us in every possible way.

Reader Three: May we live a long life and give you praise in all we do or say.

All: Amen.

If possible, show a photo of a shofar, or draw one. Ideally, you might ask a Jewish friend or neighbor to show and demonstrate a real shofar.

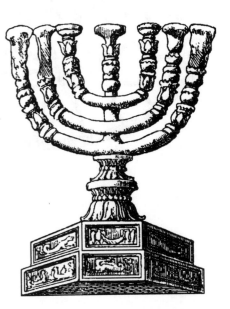

5 Grandparent's Day

Grandparent Flowers

Give children pieces of white drawing paper and ask them to draw a vase. (If some of the vases look like milk buckets, washtubs, or whatever, don't worry! Praise them to the sky. After all, as Saint Peter said, "If God approves, who am I to pass judgment?")

Then, on the board or on a poster write: "Grandmothers are…." In a second column write: "Grandfathers are…." Invite the children to give descriptive words for each column as you write them in.

Now have the children print on the vases "My Grandparents" and draw flowers to fill the vases, one flower for each descriptive word that fits their grandparents. (Have them do this even if their grandparents are deceased.)

When all the "vases" are filled with flowers, invite children to hold up their completed vases and to pray spontaneous prayers for their grandparents. Be sure to include all the grandparents in the world, especially those who may not be loved, cared for, or respected.

Loving Our Grandparents

Have the children fold a piece of white poster paper (or newsprint, if your funds are low) into fourths. In two of the squares have them print "Grandma," in the other two, "Grandpa." Do this for both sets of grandparents (maternal and paternal, whether deceased or not).

Then explain that grandparents are sometimes cheerful, kind, and loving, but sometimes they are not. Yet, God wants us to love and respect our grandparents—no matter what.

In the first square, have them draw Grandma on a good day; in the second square, have them draw Grandma on a bad day. Do the same for Grandpa and for the second set of grandparents. Next, have a short discussion with the children about what constitutes a "good day." Then invite a few of the negatives that make a "bad day."

For example, grandparents sometimes have good days because: 1) They feel well enough to get things done. 2) They get a phone call from a grandchild. Grandparents sometimes have bad days because: 1) They may be tired. 2) They may be sad because they can't see or hear well and can't accomplish what they used to. Finally, ask the children to think of additional reasons.

Invite the children to hold both posters over their hearts, as you pray:

Kind and loving God, / you love me just as I am, / sometimes cheerful, sometimes not. / Please help me to love my grandparents / just the same way: as they are. / I ask this in the name of Jesus. / Amen.

☀ Yom Kippur

Have the following words on a large piece of poster board or newsprint: Reconciliation (getting right with God and others), Atonement (to make up for wrongdoing), Synagogue (a building or place where Jewish people worship and study), Temple (a building for the worship of God), Repent (to be sorry for).

On sentence strips, write the words or phrases at the bottom left of this page. These strips should be of different lengths so that you can build a "temple" with them by pinning them on your bulletin board, one above the other, longest at the bottom (as at bottom left).

Tell the children that you will now build a "temple" to honor God, as our Jewish brothers and sisters will be honoring God in their temples and synagogues on Yom Kippur.

Take strip 1 ("Ask forgiveness from others"), and pin it at the bottom of the bulletin board. Have the children close their eyes and think of someone from whom they need forgiveness, and then invite them to ask God for the courage to ask that person for forgiveness.

Put strip 2 ("Ask forgiveness from God") above strip 1 to begin building your "temple." Have the children think of one sin they plan to ask forgiveness for the next time they receive the sacrament of reconciliation.

Add strip 3 ("Do no work"). Explain that as Catholics, Sunday is our day to focus on God and to "do no work."

Add strip 4 ("Attend services"). Talk about the importance of worship and of attending Mass regularly. Explain that it is our right and our privilege to worship God.

Add strip 5 ("Repent"). Ask children to think of one thing that they have done that they are truly sorry for. Then, have them close their eyes, recall that Jesus is present, and say the best Act of Contrition (traditional or otherwise) ever!

Add strip 6 ("Fast"). It will depend on your time whether or not you want to explain what fasting means at this point. For a shortcut, just tell children that "to fast" means to give up something, including bad habits, for the love of God and others.

Now, give each child a little slip of paper and have each write one thing they might "fast" from: an item of food, an hour of TV, wasting food, being sloppy with homework, etc. Move in procession to your prayer table and have children place their slips on it. Then pray together:

Holy God/we honor you with our "temple." / Please bless our Jewish brothers and sisters / and help us to remember your poor. / We ask this in Jesus' name. / Amen.

| FAST |
| REPENT |
| ATTEND SERVICES |
| DO NO WORK |
| ASK FORGIVENESS FROM GOD |
| ASK FORGIVENESS FROM OTHERS |

7 Triumph of the Cross

Teacher Info

For the long term: Encourage the children to make a "finger cross" whenever bad things happen to them along the way, to pray to Jesus crucified, and then to try to see if good can come out of the bad for them. This will help them always to look for little resurrections after some of the crucifixions in their young lives.

The feast of the Triumph of the Cross is observed on September 14.

Honoring the cross of Jesus goes back to the year 326, when St. Helena, mother of Emperor Constantine, is said to have found the cross of Jesus.

Have the children form a cross by bending the index finger straight down and placing the thumb against it. (I learned this from Mexican children I taught in El Paso, Texas.) Then ask: "Is the cross a good thing?" (Some will automatically respond "yes.") Look puzzled and ask: "But, can a cross that Jesus suffered and died on be a good thing?" (Some will automatically respond "no.") Now ask: "How many say yes?... How many say no?" Before a shouting match develops, say, "Hold it! You are all correct. The answer is both yes and no!"

Explain that, in a way, the cross is bad, because it was an instrument of suffering for Jesus, but it is also good, because, though Jesus died on the cross, he rose again and we can now live with him forever. Thus the cross is a sign of triumph and victory. Jesus was willing to go through something bad in order for something good to happen. He was teaching us a very important life lesson.

Now invite the children to close their eyes and think of something hard they have gone through. (Pause.)

Then ask them to try to remember if something good came out of that bad experience. Invite sharing, but let this be completely optional, always respecting privacy. You might want to share an experience from your own life to get them started.

At this point, hold up a cross or crucifix and have the children lift their arms high in the direction of the cross as you pray:

Jesus, Savior, / thank you for suffering and dying on the cross for us / and...THANK YOU for rising again! / Amen.

(Have children repeat this prayer after you a few times and encourage them to say "THANK YOU" as enthusiastically as they want.)

8 Our Lady of Sorrows

Teacher Info

This feast (September 15) has been celebrated since the seventeenth century. That's relatively recent compared to the celebration of the Seven Joys of Our Lady, called the Franciscan Crown, which was celebrated as early as 1422.

In our day, when there seems to be so much sorrow, even in the lives of children, it is good to consider how someone like Mary handled sorrow and turned it into something precious and good for God's kingdom.

Beforehand make sentence strips with these traditional seven sorrows of Our Lady printed on them (or you can write them on the board or on a big poster): The Prophecy of Simeon (Luke 2:25–38), The Flight into Egypt (Matthew 2:13–21), Losing Jesus in the Temple for Three Days (Luke 2:41–50), Meeting Jesus on the Way to Calvary (Matthew 27:31–61), Standing Beneath the Cross (John 19:25–27), Receiving the Body of Jesus from the Cross (Luke 23:26–56), The Burial of Jesus (John 19:17–42).

Pick up the sentence strip with the first of Mary's seven sorrows. Then choose children who will depict Mary, Joseph, Anna the prophetess, and Simeon. Read or paraphrase the scripture verses (making them as simple as possible), so the children will readily understand them. Then ask the four children to role-play the passage for the rest of the class as you read it. Repeat this process for all seven sorrows, changing the "cast" for each.

Children like this activity because they can be in a "play" without having to memorize too much. This activity can also easily be applied to parables, mysteries of the rosary, and other themes.

To review the seven sorrows of Mary more briefly, simply hold up the sentence strips one at a time and explain to children what each means. After each explanation, pray these words together:

"Holy Mary, mother of God, pray for us sinners, now and at the hour of our death. Amen."

Helpful Hint

This activity might work well as a lenten program for parents. Have the children take roles (in tableaux fashion) that portray as simply as possible each of the seven sorrows. Be sure the scenes are spaced several feet apart. Then have all present move in procession from one "sorrow" to the next, as a brief scripture message is proclaimed (use the passages cited above).

This is an inexpensive, yet moving portrayal of scripture, aimed at giving a good spiritual experience to both performers and audience, and it takes very little practice. I would leave the costuming up to the children, just checking that all is appropriate.

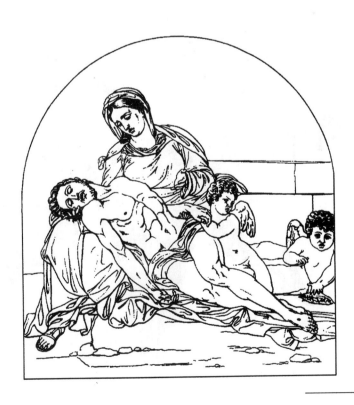

❀ Sapphire Birthdays

The birthstone for September is the sapphire, a lovely gem of a clear, deep-blue color. Show children a photo of it, if available.

After leading the children to an appreciation of God's goodness in creating such a beautiful gem, ask: "How many here have birthdays in September?" Children love birthdays, as you know.

Then, put a large piece of newsprint on a bulletin board or on a wall or in any convenient place. With a deep-blue felt pen or crayon, make a huge "gem" on the paper. Since I can't draw very well, I usually just make a big five- or six-sided figure on the paper and call it a "gem."

Inside the gem, put the names of all the children with September birthdays and put the special date under each name. After all the names are written in, print "MARY" in large letters and put an "8" under it.

Now, ask: "Who do think that is?" Possible answers, "Your mother? Your grandmother? A friend? The queen of England?"

Walk over slowly to a hiding place and with great ceremony take out a picture of Our Lady, or walk over to the class statue of Our Lady, and identify her as the mystery birthday lady.

When the din of surprise dies down, invite everyone to gather around the picture or statue of Mary to sing "Happy Birthday" to her. Then sing happy birthday to everyone in the class who has a September birthday.

Put the newsprint in a special place and encourage everyone to pray for God's blessings on the birthday people all during September.

Close this activity with a brief prayer of thanksgiving (have the children repeat it after you):

Dear God, / thank you for giving us special days / like birthdays. / Thank you for giving us Mary, / the mother of Jesus, / as our mother, too. / Thank you for the gift of life / you have given to each person here / who has a September birthday. / Amen.

10 Michaelmas Day

Teacher Info

The September flower is the aster. Aster is the Greek word for star. There are more than two hundred species of asters in North America. Each blossom is made up of two separate flowers: a little inner flower that is white or purple and a larger flower on the outside with white or blue or purple petals.

Begin this activity by asking children: "Isn't God wonderful to have thought up flowers like asters? Let's make our own asters now."

Have the children make a "little flower" with one hand and place it in the "big flower," which is the other hand. Then invite everyone to raise their "asters" on high and say, "We praise you, God, beautiful artist, for creating asters!"

Tell the children that in England, people call asters Michaelmas daisies because they often bloom on Michaelmas Day, September 29, the feast of St. Michael the Archangel.

After giving that information, go to your bulletin board and pin a large white dot in the middle of it. Pass out a large blue or purple petal to each child and have each put his or her name on the petal.

As each child goes up to pin a petal around the white center dot (forming an "aster"), lead the other children in prayer, "Thank you, God, for _____!" Everyone claps and cheers after each name is mentioned.

When all the petals are in place, have a child pin the name of Jesus in the middle of the white dot as a sign that our lives are built around Jesus. He is our inner strength. End with more clapping and cheering.

Did You Know?
In England, asters are called Michaelmas daisies because they bloom on the feast of Michael the Archangel (September 29).

OCTOBER

SUN	MON	TUES	WED	THURS	FRI	SAT

Ideas & Activities

1. Saint Therese of Lisieux
2. Guardian Angels
3. Francis of Assisi
4. Fire Prevention Week
5. Universal Children's Week
6. Our Lady of the Rosary
7. Columbus Day
8. National Dessert Day
9. Popcorn Poppin' Month
10. Halloween

✦ Saint Thérèse of Lisieux

Teacher Info

Saint Thérèse of the Child Jesus was a cloistered, Carmelite nun in Lisieux, France. Her feastday is celebrated on October 1.

A cloister is a place where persons live who have a special calling from God to pray, to fast, and to keep silence much of the day. Not everyone can do this. God has to give them special help, and God does! People who live in cloisters do what they do because they love God.

Carmelites are members of a very old religious order, dating back as far as 1452! Today, there are many kinds of Carmelites and they live all over the world.

St. Thérèse is the patron saint of missionaries. Missionaries go to foreign lands to tell about Jesus and spread the Word of God. But Thérèse stayed in one place all her life. Yet, she prayed and fasted and suffered a long illness for the intentions of missionaries. That is why she was proclaimed their patroness.

Give each child a piece of paper and have a world map in view. Have the children put a rectangle in the middle of the paper and write "St. Thérèse" in it. Then have them draw rays—long, short, middle-sized—a dozen or so. (Limit the number right away or they'll have more rays on that paper than there are countries on planet Earth!) Next, have them choose twelve countries (or whatever number limit you have decided upon), and print the names of these countries at the ends of the rays. Explain that there are probably missionaries in these countries and/or there is a need for missionaries there.

When all have completed the country names, have the children pray with you: Saint Thérèse of the Child Jesus, pray for all missionaries, especially those in _____ (here have each child name one country from his or her paper).

Finally have the children hold their papers high as they process with you to your class prayer table. Have the children place their papers on the table and then pray silently for missionaries and all the people they work with.

After class invite the children to take their papers home to keep in a special place as a reminder to pray for missionaries and for children in foreign lands.

Did You Know?

After her death, St. Thérèse was nicknamed the Little Flower. During her lifetime she promised that she would send flowers of blessings upon all those she loved. The name also fits her because she was only fifteen when she entered the convent. Like a delicate flower, her body had a hard time adjusting to the damp, cold conditions in the convent, and she eventually developed (and died from) tuberculosis. Finally, Thérèse firmly believed that doing "little" deeds of love and caring is as important as any big things we can do for God.

2 Guardian Angels

Teacher Info

In the sixteenth century, Spain celebrated a feast in honor of guardian angels, and in 1608, Pope Paul V made it a feast day in the whole church. In 1670, Pope Clement X established October 2 as the Feast of the Guardian Angels. Our guardian angels protect us from spiritual and physical dangers and help us to do good.

The Catechism of the Catholic Church says that an angel stands beside each believer as a protector, offering watchful care and intercession (336).

Ask children: "Can you see your guardian angel?" (Some children will look under their desks, in their desks, in their books, everywhere, and return to attention with a mischievous, "Nope! No angels around here!")

Then ask: "Does that mean they don't exist?" (Invite responses.) Then continue: "Just because we can't see them doesn't mean they aren't here. We can't see the air, but it's here. We know that angels exist because God revealed their existence in the bible. The church teaches that our guardian angels protect us in spiritual and physical dangers."

Then write "Physical Dangers" and "Spiritual Dangers" on the board or have two colorful signs with these words on them.

Invite children to name items that fit under each column. They probably won't have trouble naming physical dangers, but you might have to suggest a few spiritual dangers: telling lies, cheating, missing Mass, etc.

When you have completed the lists, give each of the children an envelope. On it ask them to write the words: "To my Guardian Angel." Then they should put the envelopes aside and take out a "pretend" piece of paper. Ask them to think of ways they need to be protected by their guardian angels. Then have them "write" on their pretend papers one spiritual danger and one physical danger from which they need protection. Tell them to use "invisible ink" for this.

After a reasonable time, direct them to put the pretend piece of paper in the envelope. All move to your prayer table and have children hold their envelopes as they repeat this prayer after you:

Angel of God, my guardian dear, / to whom God's love commits me here, / ever this day, be at my side, / to light, to guard, / to rule and guide. / Amen.

Encourage children to take their envelopes home and place them somewhere visible as a reminder to pray often to their guardian angels.

❸ Francis of Assisi

We associate St. Francis of Assisi with his love for God and his conversations with birds and animals. But, I also like to connect Francis with this incident that happened at the little church of San Damiano.

After his conversion, Francis was praying. He heard Jesus say to him, "Francis, rebuild my church!" Francis couldn't move fast enough. He didn't even stop to ask Jesus, "With what?" He just ran out of that church to see what he could do about rebuilding it. Remember, Francis didn't have a thing to work with. At that point, he was very poor.

So, what did he do? He begged everybody for some big rocks so he could rebuild the church. He sweated and tugged those rocks up to the church all day. People thought he'd gone nuts, but Francis didn't care. His heart was joyful to be doing something for Jesus.

The next time Francis went to pray, he listened very carefully. In his heart and mind, he heard Jesus say, "Francis, my Francis, I didn't mean to rebuild this little church, but my whole church, all over the world!"

Oops! St. Francis had made a mistake! But this time he understood. He flew out of that church as fast as he had the first time and began to preach the message of Jesus.

His feast day is observed on October 4.

After sharing the St. Francis story with your class, give each child a small stone. (If possible, take them outside and allow them to find their own stones.) Once each has a stone, say the following: "Hold your stone in the palm of your hand. As you look at it, imagine that it is a symbol of the biggest mistake you have ever made, perhaps one that really embarrassed you, one that you will never forget. Take a few moments of silence to recall what that mistake was." (Allow thirty seconds or so, and be sure to have a nice big stone in your own hand!) Then continue.

"No matter how big they are, Jesus forgives our mistakes, our faults, and our failings. He understands our weakness, but he loves us just the same. Now, turn your stone over, away from the mistakes of the past, and think for a minute about what Jesus wants you to do from now on. How can you begin anew to build up his church?" (Examples might include: telling someone a story about Jesus; showing that you are a follower of Jesus by how you act; inviting someone to go to church with you; reading the bible for someone or with someone; praying with your family.)

"Look at your rocks now in a new way, no longer as the symbol of a mistake, but as a symbol of what we can do to spread the message of Jesus. Spend a minute talking to Jesus in your own words about what you can do." (Pause.)

Finally, invite children to process to your class prayer table and place their stones there. Then have them fold their hands as you pray together:

Good St. Francis / thank you for showing us / how to change the mistakes we make / into something beautiful / that will help us spread the message of Jesus. / Amen.

Helpful Hint:

Children love to pray using guided imagery. The example used here is a simple way to invite them into the process. It's always good to allow them time to talk to God or Jesus in their own words. Try to find ways to do this on a regular basis. You won't be sorry.

✦ Fire Prevention Week

Teacher Info

When I first spotted Fire Prevention Week on the October calendar, I wasn't sure that it was relevant to catechesis.

Then I suddenly remembered a quote from Dr. Nathan Jones: "Religious educators share with other educators a common responsibility for the quality of all education taking place in our society." (Sadly, Dr. Jones died in the spring of 1994. May he rest in peace! What a loss to the field of catechetics.)

His quote inspired me to get busy thinking about how to relate Fire Prevention Week to my religion class. I came up with the activity on this page.

Note: Before the children arrive, draw a huge flame—I mean huge!—on a piece of poster board (or on a cut-open brown grocery bag). Use colored chalk or magic markers to color the flame orangy-red.

Helpful Hint

As teachers, we often ask questions, and in every group there are children who want to yell out their answers. To avoid this, establish from the start that you would like questions answered with silent gestures—as used in the activity above. Devise your own gestures or motions with input from your class. This is a great way to maintain order.

Once you have established that Fire Prevention Week is your topic, tell the children that you are going to write statements on the board. If the answer is "yes," they are to stand and put both hands on their heads. If the answer is "no," they are to stay seated and shake their heads "no."

Write: Fire is GOOD! (Half of the children will probably think "no," half will think "yes.")

Write: Fire is BAD! (The response will probably be similar to the first statement.)

Now move slowly and mysteriously to one end of the board and write the words: paper, house, forest, animal home. Ask: "If fire destroys these, is it good or bad?" (Again, ask for silent responses, as above.)

Without speaking, walk slowly to the other side of the board and write: a steak on the grill, a fire in the fireplace, a roasting marshmallow. Ask: "If fire is used for these things is it good or bad?" (Silent responses.)

Once you have established that fire can be either good or bad, explain that Fire Prevention Week reminds us that God wants us to take precaution against the bad effects of fire. God gave us wonderful minds so that we could think up ways to protect ourselves and those we love from these harmful aspects.

Point to your flame and explain that fire also gives light and warmth and is a symbol of God's love for us. Now invite the children to come forward one at a time and write their names inside the flame. Then conclude with this closing prayer:
Look after us, Creator-God, / protect us all, we pray. / If fire should endanger us / on some unhappy day, / protect our homes and families, / our forests and our lands. / We place all these together, God, / into your loving hands. / Amen.

5 Universal Children's Week

Teacher Info

Rather than focusing on what you can do for the children in your class, focus instead on what you can receive from them. What do they have to give; what is their ministry?

Cardinal Newman once said, "God has created me to do some definite service; God has committed some work to me which has not been committed to anyone else. God has not created me for nothing. I shall do good. I shall do God's work…." This is true for adults, and it's also true for children. Jesus has a special ministry for children, and we can help them discover it.

Beforehand, write these "Gifts of Children" on the board (or on sentence strips or a poster): respect, gratitude, obedience, listening, making home happy, making school happy. Explain the words as needed. Then ask: "Does anyone know what ministry means?" The likely response will be "no." Explain that it is the act of serving, and since you are a catechist—religion teacher—you are serving God and the church by telling the class about Jesus, by teaching religion.

Then ask children: "What is your ministry? In what way do you serve?" (Great pause!) Direct their attention to the Gifts of Children that you have posted, and invite comments. Then, using your name cards (see activity 1 in September), divide the class into small groups, and assign one of the gifts to each group. Ask them to come up with as many ways to practice this gift as there are fingers on their left hand (using the left hand gets their attention).

Then, bring the class together again and share in the following way: One person from each group reports by saying: "Children can give the gift of respect by…." (He or she should then read the five items that the particular group has decided upon). Go through all six gifts this way.

Finally, you might want to close the session with this reflection: "So often, people think that children like you don't have a ministry. We have seen today that you have many wonderful ways to serve. Together, let us pray about this happy news." Have everyone move to the prayer table and repeat after you:

Holy and gracious God / thank you for giving us a ministry / a way to serve God, the church, and others. / Please help us to do it well. / Amen.

Did You Know:

The *Catechism of the Catholic Church* lists these six "Gifts of Children":

1) Respect for parents; 2) Gratitude for the gift of life and for love; 3) Obedience to parents and (aha!) to teachers; 4) Listening to "reasonable directions" of parents and teachers; 5) Making home happy by good relationships with brothers and sisters; 6) Gratitude to grandparents, other members of the family, pastors, catechists, and other teachers and friends.

☀ Our Lady of the Rosary

Have available for this activity a large rosary (or at least a brightly colored one) and five large pieces of newsprint (cut-open brown grocery bags work, too). Beforehand print the Joyful Mysteries on the board or on a poster. Give each child a large piece of paper. If the children are familiar with the rosary, great! If not, introduce them to it. Place your rosary in a conspicuous place and ask them to imitate it by drawing in (using their favorite colors) all of the "Hail Mary's" and "Glory Be's."

Now comes the best part! With great pizzazz put the five pieces of newsprint (or grocery bags) on the floor. That's right, children love to work on the floor! Divide them into five equal groups and assign one of the Joyful Mysteries to each group to illustrate as creatively as they can. Be sure they include the name of the mystery. Invite one child from each group to explain to the class what the group has drawn. Hang this finished work of art in a visible place, perhaps even in your parish church.

Here are a few other ways to introduce children to the mysteries of the rosary:

1) Take your class outdoors and make a huge rosary in the grass, using pebbles for the beads and twigs for the crucifix. Then have the children act out the mysteries in the center of this "rosary," while a short, appropriate scriptural passage is read. Before closing, say a decade of the rosary together.

2) Ask your local appliance store for one of the huge boxes that a TV or washing machine comes in. Have the children draw the mysteries of the rosary on the four sides and top. When you tire of looking at it, turn the box upside down and invite the children to take turns stepping into it for puppet presentations about the mysteries of the rosary (sock or paper bag puppets work fine for this).

3) Go to the shoe store and get fifteen shoe boxes. Have the children make shadow boxes, one for each of the fifteen mysteries. Exhibit these for other students—even for the whole parish.

4) Make a "movie" about the mysteries of the rosary. Use two rolling pins or cardboard rollers and enough newsprint or butcher paper to draw all of the mysteries. Then, have a "meditation" as each mystery unrolls, asking: 1) What does this mystery portray? 2) What can we learn from it? 3) How can we share what we have learned? Helping children to develop a love for the rosary in these ways will never be time wasted.

⑦ Columbus Day

Teacher Info

Columbus Day can teach us that when things don't end up as we planned, it's not necessarily bad. Consider the following:

Around 1492, the Ottoman Turks had cut off easy access to Asian goods from the countries of Europe. That was bad! But that forced Europeans to try to find new routes to Asia, and they ended up doing a lot of exploring and found new lands. That was good!

Columbus didn't find the route he was looking for. That was bad! But he ended up making a lasting connection between East and West. That was good!

The Europeans had a great desire to spread Christianity. But Columbus, who was a Catholic, didn't act much like a Christian in the way he treated the natives of the Western lands. That was bad! But, in spite of that, Christianity did spread. That was good!

As we celebrate Columbus Day, we can look at our own lives and see that though things don't always turn out as planned, something good can come of it.

For this activity, have available for each child a business-sized envelope (#10), or a pocket made by folding a piece of paper and stapling the sides. You will also need pieces of paper, one for each child, that will fit into the envelope when folded in thirds.

Now, write on the board: "Plans We Sometimes Make," and offer these examples: going on a picnic, climbing a tree, cleaning under the bed, writing a letter, going to the mall, beginning a garden, going swimming or fishing, planning a school project, making a present for someone. Explain that all of these are plans we sometimes make and all of them might turn out as expected—or they might not. Look together at going on a picnic, for example. Possible outcomes are: We enjoy the picnic; it rains; we get lost on the way.

Enjoying the picnic is obviously good, but explain that rain, though not good for a picnic, gives needed water to plants and trees and gardens, which is good. Even getting lost can turn out okay if we find a better picnic spot or if we suddenly meet people we know who are also going on a picnic and who ask us to join them.

Now, give each child an envelope (or pocket) and have them choose one of the plans from the board and print it on the front of the envelope. Next, give each the piece of paper and have them fold it in thirds. (Be sure to demonstrate how to do this!) Direct the children to write three possible outcomes of the plan they have chosen. Then, one at a time, have them come up and read the plan and its outcomes. Challenge the class to put a positive spin on each outcome. When all have had a turn, conclude with the following Columbus Day prayer (as you pray, have children hold up their envelopes):

Gracious God / thank you for holidays / and for people like Christopher Columbus / who made great discoveries. / Thank you, too, for all the surprises / you give us in our lives. / When things don't turn out as we plan / please help us to see the good / in whatever does happen. / We ask this in Jesus' name. / Amen.

National Dessert Day

Teacher Info

Beforehand, clip as many pictures of desserts as possible from old magazines. Also have pieces of paper available, one sheet for each child. Have two colorful sentence strips prepared that read:

1) God dwells in us;

2) God wants us to take care of ourselves.

Finally, arrange for volunteer parents to bring in a surprise dessert at the end of this lesson.

National Dessert Day is observed on October 14.

To get started, invite the children to study the dessert pictures and have each choose one that especially appeals to them. Have them paste these on the top half of their papers. On the bottom half, have them write a brief original prayer asking God to help them to use good things, like dessert, in moderation.

National Dessert Day is a great occasion to remind children that God gives us good things, but that we must use them wisely. Sometimes "good" things can be bad for us. Ask for examples. When can eating too much be bad for us and why? When can eating salty or fatty foods be bad for us? Are some desserts fatty or salty? What desserts are probably the most healthy?

After this discussion, invite the children to share some of their favorite desserts as illustrated on their papers. When all have shared their papers, explain that one of God's commandments (the Fifth Commandment), reminds us to take good care of our bodies and our health. (At this point show the sentence strips and have children read them aloud together.)

Now move to your prayer corner and invite each child to complete the following phrase by naming their favorite dessert: "Thank you, God for _____." After all have had a turn, pray this closing prayer together:

Good and gracious God, / we thank you for the gift of food, / especially desserts. / We ask you to help us / to use food in good ways / because you dwell in us, / and you want us to care for ourselves. / Amen.

Now enjoy the special dessert provided by parent volunteers!

Popcorn Poppin' Month

Teacher Info

Did you know that October is Popcorn Poppin' Month? Popcorn is one of the oldest forms of corn. Native Americans grew popcorn for thousands of years before people from Europe arrived in North and South America in the fifteenth and sixteenth centuries. Native Americans used popcorn for food, but they also used it for decorations and in their religious ceremonies.

Popcorn has a hard shell, but the inside is soft and moist. When popcorn is heated to 204°, the kernel bursts and a white, fluffy substance pops out.

If possible have available a large bowl of popped popcorn and a small container of unpopped popcorn for this activity.

Give each child a popped kernel and an unpopped kernel. Ask them not to eat it, but to hold it in their hands.

Then say: "Look at the unpopped kernel. Do you know that, although the outside is very hard, the inside is soft and moist? Can you tell this just by looking at the unpopped kernel?" Invite the children to comment.

Then continue: "In a way, people are a little like popcorn. Just think for a minute about someone you don't like: a family member, a neighbor, a classmate, a teacher. (Pause.) Could it be that you don't really know this person? Could it be that this person might be very different on the inside than on the outside?

"Now close your eyes and try to think of one good thing about that person. Everyone has some good qualities. Hold the unpopped popcorn in your hand. As you begin to think of something good about the person, pretend that the kernel's heating up. Keep thinking of good things about that person until he or she doesn't seem so bad after all. When that happens—pow! That person begins to look more like a beautiful piece of popped popcorn, like the piece in your hand. Hold up your beautiful popped kernel."

Conclude with this prayer:

Good and gracious God / we thank you for popcorn / and we thank you / for all the beautiful symbols / we can find in popcorn / to remind us that you are good / and that you love us very much. / Amen.

Now invite the children to share the bowl of popcorn.

Helpful Hint

Note that this exercise can also be used for *things* that children dislike: a class, a subject, a food—anything.

It can also be used with many different topics like baptism or reconciliation—or any of the sacraments, really—to symbolize the passing over from life on earth with Jesus to life in eternity with Jesus. You can use it for Holy Week: Jesus in the tomb (unpopped kernel), then Jesus resurrected (popped kernel). Did you suspect that the lowly popcorn had so many "evangelization" possibilities?

10 Halloween

Tell the children that you will be reading a list of good and bad things that children might do on Halloween. Direct them to hold their bags in their hands. When you read a good thing, they should turn the good face on the bag toward you. When you read a bad thing, they should turn the monster face toward you.

(NOTE: When using the suggested list below, or coming up with your own list, be sure to name more good behaviors than bad.)

Suggested list of behaviors:
- Help younger children on Halloween night (good).
- Be more quiet at the house of elderly neighbors (good).
- Destroy property (bad).
- Share your treats with someone (good).
- Fuss at your parents because you don't like your costume (bad).
- Say please and thank you every time you get a treat (good).
- Don't push or shove (good).
- Be careful not to walk on people's lawns and flowers (good).
- Run across the street without looking both ways (bad).
- Steal candy from someone (bad).
- Thank everyone who helped you to have a good time (good).

After you have finished your list, invite the children to take turns standing before the group to name additional good actions they might do on Halloween.

When all have had a turn, ask everyone to stand and face the class prayer table. Lead them in this prayer:

Precious God, /thank you for a day like Halloween. /We just love it! / Please help us to behave / so that we will all have a wonderful time. / And please help all those children in the world / who are sad or suffering on this day. / Amen.

NOVEMBER

SUN	MON	TUES	WED	THURS	FRI	SAT

Ideas & Activities

1. All Saints Day
2. All Souls Day
3. National Moms' and Dads' Day
4. Saint Rose Duchesne
5. Homemade Bread Day
6. Thanksgiving Day
7. Advent
8. Martin de Porres
9. Saint Cecilia
10. Election Day

✦ All Saints Day

Begin this activity by asking children if they have ever heard of the communion of saints. Those who have should put both their hands on their head. Those who haven't should make a big zero with their fingers. (These responses should be done in silence to avoid disruption and shouting out.) Invite those children who have heard of the communion of saints to share their understanding with the class.

When it's your turn, explain that just as holy communion means a close relationship with Jesus, "communion" in the communion of saints means a close relationship among the people of God in heaven, the people of God in purgatory, and the people of God on earth. We are all united in Jesus.

Next, divide the children into three groups, symbolizing: 1) People in heaven; 2) People in purgatory; and 3) People on earth. Have group one move to your class prayer corner and lift their hands to heaven in an attitude of prayer, while you announce: "The people of God in heaven are praying *for* the people of God in purgatory and on earth. That's what happens when we pray to the saints."

Now have group two move to the prayer corner and do the same as you announce: "The people of God in purgatory pray *to* God for the people of God on earth (that's us!), and they pray *with* the people of God in heaven." Finally, group three should move to the prayer corner and stand, arms high, in an attitude of prayer. Announce: "We, the people of God on earth, pray *with* the people of God in heaven, and *for* the people of God in purgatory."

When the children get back to their places, demonstrate these relationships by pointing to your triangle and discussing it. End this activity by singing a resounding hymn like "In Christ There Is No East or West" or "For All the Saints." Invite the children to process around the room as they sing.

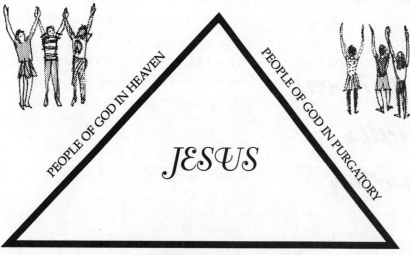

2 All Souls Day

Teacher Info

In the seventh century, monks began offering Mass on the day after Pentecost for their departed community members. In 988, the Benedictine monastery of Cluny began celebrating a feast to remember all of their dead on November 2. This practice spread to other monasteries and eventually to parishes served by secular clergy.

In the thirteenth century, Rome placed the feast day on the annual calendar for the universal church. The same date was kept so that all of the departed members of the church as the communion of saints might be remembered on successive days, the triumphant saints in heaven on November 1, and those in purgatory on November 2.

Helpful Hint

All Souls Day is a complicated feast to present to children because of the danger of confusing "souls" with the ghosts of Halloween. Early in my teaching career, I learned not to put adult thinking into children's heads—it doesn't work. So though I tried to learn more about the concept of "soul" for my own benefit, I didn't attempt to get into it too deeply with the children. When I was a young teacher, in the days when we prayed "Father, Son, and Holy Ghost," I asked the children to illustrate how they perceived each of the three persons. Sure enough, they drew ghosts for the Holy Spirit. Today, the **Catechism of the Catholic Church** gives us tremendous help for our own education concerning "soul" (see paragraphs 362-368).

In preparation for this activity, prepare three sentence strips. On the first write: "Know God"; on the second write: "Love God"; and on the third write: "Serve God." These should be written in bright colors. Also prepare three "signs" that read "My House," "My Friend's Porch," "My Friend's House."

Begin by explaining to the children that on All Souls Day we remember those people who tried to be good friends of God during their lifetimes. They really tried to know God (hold up card one), love God (card two), and serve God (card three). But when they died, they were not quite ready for the glory of heaven. (The *Catechism* says it this way: "All who die in God's grace and friendship, but still imperfectly purified, are indeed assured of their eternal salvation; but after death they undergo purification, so as to achieve the holiness necessary to enter the joy of heaven" [#1030]).

The following brief skit offers children an analogy (admittedly, an imperfect one, but look what St. Patrick did with a shamrock!). Invite three children to come forward. One holds the sign "My House." The middle child holds the sign "My Friend's Porch." The third child holds the sign "My Friend's House." Have the first two stand at some distance from one another. Then have another child come up and role-play as you say the following (slowly to allow sufficient time for the role-play): "After I left my house—on the way to my friend's house—I went through some mud and got lots of it on my shoes. I didn't want to go into my friend's house with mud on my shoes, so I stayed on the porch until I could get the mud off my shoes. Once my shoes were clean I went in and played with my friend." Explain that Purgatory is somthing like that.

Conclude by moving to your prayer table to pray the following for the "souls" in purgatory. Have children repeat each line after you:

Gracious and loving God, / all the people in purgatory / are your friends and ours. / Help them to go to heaven soon. / Dear holy people of God in Purgatory, / you are God's friends. / Please pray to God for us / so that we will know God, / love God, / and serve God / all our lives. / This we ask in the name of Jesus. / Amen.

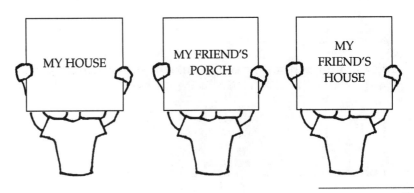

3 National Moms' and Dads' Day

For this activity you will need a good-sized kettle (cooking pot), a large wooden spoon, and a good pile of 6" x 2" paper strips, at least one for each child.

After your opening prayer, bring out the kettle and place it on your desk. I guarantee it will get children's attention! Explain: "In my magic kettle, we are going to mix all kinds of ingredients that make up a good Christian family. Some possible ingredients are love, respect, good communication, forgiveness, patience, family prayer, and family meals, but I'd like you to think of as many as you can and write them on one of these strips." (Each "ingredient" should be on a separate strip.)

When all have finished, have the children fold the papers and drop them into the kettle. Stir them with your big wooden spoon.

Then invite the children to come forward one by one, draw out a strip, and read the message on it. When all have been read, ask: "Do all of our families have all of these ingredients?" Explain that none of our families are perfect, but that we can work together to make them better.

Finally, give children pieces of paper and invite them to write down the ingredients that they *wish* their families had. Then have them fold the papers and hold them over their hearts as you lead them in the following prayer:

Good and loving God / please bless all the families in the world. / Help them to grow in love and care. (Invite the children to ask God, in silence, for the needs of their own families. Pause for a few moments while they do this and then conclude.) We ask this in the name of Jesus, / our brother and friend. / Amen.

4 Saint Rose Duchesne

For this activity, put together several chairs, desks, tables, or whatever is available, to form a large oblong shape. That's your steamboat! Now, choose four children and have them pretend that they are boarding the steamboat with their luggage. One of them should be St. Rose. (Also appoint a child to be the reporter referred to below.)

Tell the children the steamboat story about St. Rose Philippine Duchesne and explain that she could easily have wasted a whole week by being angry and frustrated. Instead, she used the time to pray so that when she got to St. Louis, her work could be a success and many would come to know, love, and serve God.

Now have the participating children pretend that the steamboat is sailing along smoothly when—bang!—it hits a sandbar. Have the "reporter" come aboard the steamboat with pen and pad to ask the stranded passengers what they plan to do for a whole week, since they won't be allowed to leave the ship. Invite children to make up answers, for example, "I'm going to sleep all week!" "I'm going to read a pile of books." When the interviewer asks St. Rose, she should say, "I'm going to make a retreat."

Reporter: "And what is that?"

Rose Duchesne: "It's spending time praying to God and listening to God. I'm glad to have this unexpected time. I may be too busy later."

When the steamboat is freed, everyone goes ashore (and the room gets put back in order.) Invite the children to discuss the role-play and the concept of spending time in retreat, listening to and talking to God. Encourage them to spend quiet "mini-retreat" moments at home as often as they can.

For your closing prayer, invite the children to respond with this refrain: "Help us to _____ well."

Teacher: When it's time to play, dear Jesus…

Children: Help us to play well.

Teacher: When it's time to study, dear Jesus…

Children: Help us to study well.

Teacher: When it's time to pray, dear Jesus…

Children: Help us to pray well.

Add as many petitions as you like and then conclude as follows:

Our good and gracious God, / please help us to use our time well, / doing everything for your honor and glory, / as St. Rose Philippine Duchesne did. / Help us to lead many people / to know, love, and serve you. / Amen.

5 Homemade Bread Day

Teacher Info
Bread has existed since pre-historic days, and it is the most widely eaten food in the world in one form or another. It is possible, say historians, that Egyptians might have been making yeast bread as long ago as 2600 B.C. The Egyptians taught bread-making to the Greeks, who taught it to the Romans. By 100 A.D. or so, most of Europe was making bread.

By the Middle Ages, most of Europe had bread-bakeries. At first people ate only wheat or whole-grain bread, but in the late 1800s white flour was milled. White bread was a common food by the 1900s.

Bread has often been used as a symbol of Christian unity, and Jesus uses it to share his life with us in the holy eucharist. Homemade Bread Day is observed on November 17.

If possible, have a loaf of homemade bread to share after this activity.

Before class, move all your desks or tables to the edge of the room so that the center of the room is clear. (When the children come in, have them sit in the seats along the walls.) Also, draw a huge loaf of bread (several yards long and two feet wide) and cut it out. Have available 4" x 4" pieces of paper, one for each child.

Begin this activity by explaining that bread is used as a symbol of unity among Christians. Many grains make one loaf. Then take out your big loaf of bread and roll it out onto the middle of the floor. Give each of the children a piece of the precut paper and have them put their name on it as well as one gift they can share with the other children in class. Emphasize *qualities*, not achievements, for example: I am truthful and kind; I appreciate other people; I enjoy watching stars; I am a good friend; I am a follower of Jesus.

When the papers are finished, give each child a piece of tape or a dab of glue and have them fasten the papers to your loaf of bread. Then ask: "How many loaves of bread do we have?" (Response: "One!") "How many wonderful people?" (Response: "A lot!")

Explain that when we take part in the eucharist, which is a meal, and we receive Jesus together in communion, we all become part of Jesus and Jesus becomes part of us. We don't really know how this happens, but we know it does, because scripture says so." Illustrate by reading 1 Corinthians 10:17: "Because the loaf of bread is one, we, though many, are one body, for we all partake of the one loaf."

Finally, holding hands around the bread, have the children repeat this prayer after you:

Jesus, Bread of Life / help us to be united to you, / to one another, / and to Christians all over the world. / Amen.

Now share the homemade bread (if available).

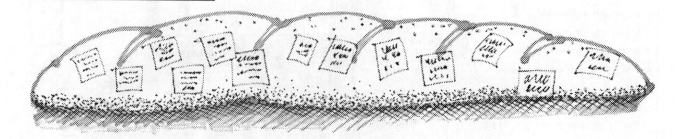

6 Thanksgiving Day

Thanksgiving rituals and celebrations have been observed since the beginning of time. Ancient peoples offered thanks to God and built rock altars for this purpose. Jesus gave thanks often, giving us an example to do the same.

Closer to our time, the first Thanksgiving Day in New England, held around 1621, was a marvelous festival that lasted three full days. There were prayers of thanksgiving to God for a good harvest, and a great feast which was held outdoors for Plymouth families and their Native American friends.

The celebration of Thanksgiving Day as a national holiday developed through the years, and the date changed back and forth until 1941 when the U.S. Congress set the date at the third Thursday of November.

For this activity you will need colorful cut-out leaves, at least one for each child, a hole-puncher, 8" pieces of yarn, and a large dry tree branch anchored in a can of sand. To begin, share with children a short history of Thanksgiving Day and initiate a discussion about all the things we can be thankful for, with emphasis on qualities and talents rather than material things.

Then lead children in a discussion about God's spiritual gifts: the eucharist, sacraments, God's love and care, prayer, Mary and the saints, guardian angels, and the church. Once you have named all these blessings, invite the children to select a few favorites and write them on their leaves. If the children have so many blessings that they need more leaves, great! Give them as many as possible. Remember, the more they give thanks in your class, the more likely they are to give thanks out of it.

Now ask the children to flip their leaves over and write a short thank-you note to God. Punch a hole through the leaf, give everyone a piece of yarn, and have them tie the yarn into a loop for hanging. Now move in procession to your prayer table and have the children hang their leaves on the tree branch. This activity can end with a formal or spontaneous prayer of thanksgiving, a prayer-poem, or a thanksgiving hymn.

Or, you can invite the children each to take a turn coming forward and praying: "Thank you, God, for_____." After each prayer, the class can respond: "For all your blessings we give thanks."

An Alternate Activity

Tell the children that though we in North America have many material gifts, many people in our world have very little. Thanksgiving is an excellent time to pray for the world's poor.

Give children pieces of *lined* paper, and ask them to choose a poor country of the world (or a poor area in your own town) and write a letter to God asking for blessings on the children there. Have children take these letters home as a reminder of their own blessings, but also as a reminder to pray for those who are in need.

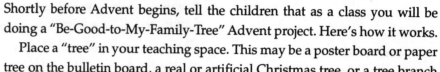

7 The Advent Season

Teacher Info

Advent begins the church's liturgical year and lasts more or less four weeks. It is observed in remembrance of the thousands of years that the chosen people anticipated the coming of the savior. The word "advent" comes from the Latin *adventus*. When I asked what *adventus* means, one child in my class said it means *adventure*. That may not be far from the truth! Actually, it means "coming or arrival," which, we have to admit is an adventure, considering who it is who comes!

Some Advent projects and celebrations are already well known to teachers and catechists, for example, the Advent wreath, Kris Kindle, the Jesse Tree, the O Antiphons, and the Advent calendar. On this page are some additional suggested activities.

Shortly before Advent begins, tell the children that as a class you will be doing a "Be-Good-to-My-Family-Tree" Advent project. Here's how it works.

Place a "tree" in your teaching space. This may be a poster board or paper tree on the bulletin board, a real or artificial Christmas tree, or a tree branch anchored in sand. Have the children cut out ornaments, either in Christmas colors or perhaps from Christmas wrapping paper. (Ornaments are easy to cut out. Just cut out a ball with a little hump on the top. Punch a hole in the little hump, slip a piece of yarn or Christmas ribbon through the hole, and tie it into a loop.) Have a gift-wrapped box available to hold these ornaments, and place the box on your prayer table.

Explain the project this way: "In preparation for Christmas, we are going to help one another find ways to make our families happy during Advent. When one of you does something at home to make others happy, you can write it on one of the ornaments and hang it on our class tree. During Advent we will spend time during each class reading our Christmas ornaments and sharing ideas about how to make our families happy." (You might want to suggest things children can do to be helpful and caring at home.)

You also might want to try building a stable with your class as a bulletin board project. First, cut out and then arrange a simple "stable" on your bulletin board, made with five long strips of dark brown paper. Put two strips on the sides, one strip on the bottom, and two strips at the top for the roof. Now give each child a piece of brown paper, 4 x 4 or so, and have them cut out a good-sized "rock" (or give them "rocks" already cut out, depending on your time), and have them decorate the rocks (cut-out brown grocery bags work fine for this). Tell children that to celebrate the birthday of Jesus, you will be building a stable shelter for him and Mary and Joseph using your rocks. Each rock will represent a good deed done for the love of Jesus during Advent.

Invite children to spend a few moments in silence to decide what their deeds will be, and then have them write at least one on the backside of their rock. After the deeds are written in, process together to your bulletin board and have the children pin their rocks (decorated side out) to the outside of the stable.

Then pray together:

Jesus our Savior / all during Advent / we will try to practice the good deeds / written on our rocks. / Thank you for coming among us. / Amen.

Other Advent Ideas

• Prepare a paper quilt for your bulletin board, making each square a picture of what loving people can do for one another to prepare for Christmas. Have children bring in pictures for this or make drawings.

• Build a "prayer home" for all the homeless people in the world, each brick representing a prayer that everyone will work together to find homes for the homeless.

• Cut out footprints (many footprints), and have them everywhere in your room: on the walls, the desks, the floor. Each symbolizes our "walk" toward the manger during Advent to remind children of the real meaning of Christmas.

8 Martin de Porres

Teacher Info

Martin de Porres was born in Lima, Peru, on November 3, 1579. His father was a Spanish soldier and his mother was a black freed-woman from Panama. Martin became a Dominican lay brother and spent his life as a farm-laborer, infirmarian, and barber. He was devoted to the sick and to the beggars who came daily to the monastery gate, and he was known for his great devotion to the holy eucharist. Martin was sometimes looked down upon because of his racial heritage, but he made the best of it and he was considered by all who knew him to be a holy man.

In the United States, Martin is known as the patron saint of those who work for interracial justice, and his feast day is November 3. St. Paul didn't know Martin de Porres, but his letter to the Colossians (Col 3:12–13), describes Martin very well—as you will see in the activity on this page.

Beforehand, draw and cut out an old "jalopy," big enough for everyone to see. Write your name and the names of all the children on it. Begin by sharing with the children a brief account of St. Martin's life. Then have one of the children read Colossians 3:12–13. Suggest that the children listen for qualities that could describe St. Martin. Hopefully, they will come up with words like: chosen, holy, beloved, merciful, kind, humble, meek, patient, and forgiving.

Now make a very long line across the board. Let's say you live in St. Louis. Write "St. Louis" at the left end of your line and "St. Martin" at the other end. Challenge the children: "Here *we* are (point to St. Louis) and here St. Martin is (point to St. Martin). Look at the *long* road we have to walk to be the kind of follower Martin was. How can *we* better follow Jesus? What did St. Paul say we have to do?"

Go to the board and write all along your line the words that you and the class came up with from Colossians. Here's where the "jalopy" comes in. Have one of the children move it along the "road" as you write each new word. Tell the children that when they find ways to imitate St. Martin de Porres, they will be moving closer to St. Martin—and to Jesus!

When you and the jalopy finally get to St. Martin, have the child who is "driving" it lead the class to your prayer space. Place the car on your prayer table and have the children extend their right hands toward it as you pray the following:

Teacher: Good St. Martin de Porres, you were a friend of Jesus and his poor…
Children: St. Martin, pray for us.
Teacher: Please help us to be kind and merciful…
Children: St. Martin, pray for us.
Teacher: Help us, too, to be patient and forgiving…
Children: St. Martin, pray for us.

Helpful Hint

When you use scripture passages with your class, always have children locate the passage in their bibles and follow along or even take turns reading it. I take it for granted that each child has a bible. Tell your DRE or principal that you can do without desks, chairs, tables, blackboards, but not without one bible per child! Ask him or her to check with a local religious bookstore or contact the American Bible Society (1865 Broadway, New York, NY 10023) for information about economical bibles for children.

Saint Cecilia

You can approach this activity in two ways:

1) If you don't mind making a spectacle of yourself (the children will be delighted if you do!), sit at your desk or table and pretend that you are playing the piano. At first the children will only be puzzled. Just keep going. Eventually, someone will ask what you are doing. They will soon guess that you are playing the piano and you'll have their attention.

2) If being silly is not in your makeup (and that's *fine*!), here is another way to begin this activity. Put on a tape, record, or CD of soft music and explain that you are beginning this activity with music because you are going to introduce them to the patron saint of music, St. Cecilia!

At this point, both approaches proceed in the same way.

After you briefly introduce Cecilia, give everyone an 8 x 11 piece of paper and explain that music is all around us in our daily lives, not just on tapes, records, and CDs, but also in God's creation. Sometimes we have to be still and listen to hear it. Offer children several examples and invite further suggestions from them. Your list might include the following: the singing of birds, the whistling of the wind, water going over rocks, the sound crickets make, thunder making drum-music. Once your list is complete, have the children choose their favorite "music" from it and write it on the paper. Invite them to take turns sharing their choices.

When all have shared, process to your class prayer corner, again playing the background music (if you used it), and have the children hold up their papers and repeat after you as you pray:

Good and gracious God / creator of music / thank you for the beautiful sounds of music. / Please help us to see / that there is music in all of your creation. / Help us to use music / for your honor and glory / and to give joy to others. / St. Cecilia, patron saint of music / pray for us. / Amen.

⭐ Election Day

Teacher Info

What does Election Day (second Tuesday in November), have to do with religion class? A lot! Let me quote from Contemporary Approaches to Christian Education by Jack L. Seymour, et al. (Nashville: Abingdon Press): "Christian education must seek to recover its historic commitment to social transformation."

No one, I believe, can argue that our society, and in particular our political fabric, doesn't need "transformation." But, how can this begin in religion class? In the same way that a tomato plant can begin from a seed. We have to convince children that we must follow Jesus in all areas of our lives, one step at a time—even the political areas.

We adults can always tell it's election time by the speeches, the promises, the whoppers, and the mud-slinging! But in case children are oblivious to all this, remind them that elections are coming up.

Begin this activity by asking: "Do you think there is anything *we* can do to make elections just and honest and good for the whole country?" Most children will probably say "no" since it is generally believed by their parents that "all politicians are crooks." Share the information below about Thomas More at this point.

Then ask: "What if *we* were all politicians? What would it take for us to be honest?" Write the word *honesty* on the board or on a poster. Then have the children help you come up with items that identify an honest politician. For example, honest politicians do not promise to do what they know can't be done; respect their opponent and do not say dishonest things; do not spend money that does not belong to them; are people who openly keep God's laws.

When your list is finished, divide the class into pairs. Have one child take the role of an honest politician and the other a dishonest politician. Have each prepare a short speech that fits his or her role. You might want to suggest "speech" subjects: promises about what they will do about education, pets, pollution, crime, drugs, etc. When the speeches are ready, have the teams come up and deliver them. Then invite the class to decide which of the politicians is honest and which is dishonest.

When all the teams have performed, together make up a prayer to St. Thomas More, asking him to help politicians and government leaders. Send this prayer to your local and diocesan newspapers and to politicians themselves. Your prayer might go something like this:

St. Thomas More, / you were a lawyer and a politician, / but you always tried to be honest and good. / Help our leaders today / to stand up for what is right / and to be honest and respectful of one another. / We ask this in Jesus' name. / Amen.

This is admittedly a small step, but assure children that if we Christians are ever to transform society, we must begin somewhere!

Did You Know?

Saint Thomas More, born in 1478, was the son of a politician and later became a politician himself. He studied law and built himself a large and profitable practice. He was elected to parliament at the age of 25 and at age 32 was appointed Under-Sheriff, a very prestigious position. He became Henry VIII's Lord Chancellor in 1532. When Henry decided to claim total power, thus denying the authority of the church, Thomas More resigned. Henry insisted that he make a public oath of loyalty, but Thomas refused, and he spent 15 months in prison. In 1535 he was executed.

Be sure to share with your class that Thomas More was an honest (and courageous) politician!

DECEMBER

SUN	MON	TUES	WED	THURS	FRI	SAT

Ideas & Activities

1. Saint Nicholas
2. Our Lady of Guadalupe
3. Saint Lucy
4. Christmas Eve
5. Christmas Day
6. Saint Stephen
7. Saint John the Evangelist
8. Feast of the Holy Innocents
9. Feast of the Holy Family
10. New Year's Eve

Saint Nicholas

Teacher Info

St. Nicholas of Myra, Asia Minor, lived in the fourth century. (We use his full title to keep him from being confused with St. Nicholas of Flue from Switzerland, St. Nicholas of Tolentino from Italy, and St. Nicholas Tavelis, who was martyred in the Holy Land.)

St. Nicholas of Myra must have been a colorful individual, because he has always been a popular saint. Most of the events reported about him are said to be legends, including the one in which St. Nicholas saved three young girls from horrible lives because their father had no dowry for them. Supposedly, St. Nicholas threw gold coins through the window at night and then rushed away so that the family would not know who the benefactor was. He didn't want to attract attention to his good deed. This harmonizes perfectly with Jesus' lesson about not letting your right hand know what the left one is doing!

The feast of St. Nicholas is observed on December 6. Before you begin the activity on this page, have available a small bag of handmade paper coins, plus extra coins, one for each child, and an old rug.

Tell the children about St. Nicholas and the three daughters, or, better yet, let them act it out. Choose one boy to play St. Nicholas, and three girls to play the poor daughters. Have the three daughters pretend to be asleep on the rug behind a row of chairs or desks (they won't mind being on the floor).

Then proceed using this short script: "In the fourth century lived St. Nicholas of Myra. (The child playing St. Nicholas carries the bag of coins and begins to move slowly to the front of the room.) Nicholas was very kind, and when he heard that three young girls were about to become homeless, because their family had no money, he sneaked down a side street with a bagful of coins. (The child moves with sneaking motions.) Nicholas pushed the money through the window of the house and ran away before anyone could see him. (The child throws the coins and runs back to the rear of the room.) The daughters discover the money and are delighted." If you have time, allow different children to take turns role-playing this scene.

Congratulate the children on their fine performances and then lead them into a discussion about the meaning of the story. Ask: "If Nicholas didn't even know those young women, why did he want to help them? Why didn't he want people to see him giving the money? What should we do about people in need (even if we don't know them)?"

Then discuss ways the children can help others, beginning with becoming more aware of the needs of those around them. Write their suggestions on the board or on a poster. Then give each of the children one of the paper coins and ask them to think about one thing they could possibly do to show more generosity to others. Once they think of one thing in particular, invite them to write their name on the coin. Have one child collect the coins and carry them to your class prayer table. Explain that these coins will represent the special gifts of love the children are doing as they await the birth of Jesus.

Close with this prayer or a similar one:

Jesus, whose birthday we will soon celebrate / help us to be thoughtful of others / as St. Nicholas was. / Give us courage to do all we can / to meet the needs of those around us. / Please help us to think of others / at least once a day / every day until Christmas. / Amen.

Our Lady of Guadalupe

Teacher Info

In 1531, as a poor Native American, Juan Diego, was hurrying over Tepeyac Hill, near Mexico City, a beautiful lady appeared to him. She asked him to go and tell Bishop Zummaraga to build a church in her honor there. Juan did as the lady told him, but, of course, the bishop didn't believe this. She appeared to him two more times. Finally, on the fourth time that the lady appeared she told Juan Diego that she wanted to be called "Our Lady of Guadalupe," and she left the imprint of her beautiful self upon Juan's cloak. When the bishop saw the imprint, he believed, and Our Lady of Guadalupe got her church.

Today, in place of the original church, there is a huge shrine-church of Our Lady of Guadalupe, to which pilgrims from all over the world go to pray. The cloak of Juan Diego is in that church in Mexico City. Our Lady of Guadalupe is called the Patroness of the Americas and her feast day is December 12.

If possible, have a large picture of Our Lady of Guadalupe on hand, either a commercial print (they are easily obtainable at church goods stores) or an "original" by an artist in your class.

"Enshrine" the picture on your prayer altar by pinning it to a large decorated box . Then cut streamers out of crepe paper in the colors of the Mexican flag: red, white, and green. Add gold for Our Lady of Guadalupe.

To begin this activity, tell the children the story of Our Lady of Guadalupe. Then teach them this brief prayer: "Nuestra Señora de Guadalupe, Raga por nos otros" (Our Lady of Guadalupe, pray for us). Practice it several times until the children feel comfortable praying it.

Next, give each of the children a streamer to be taped to the end of their ruler. (If you don't have rulers use twigs. If that isn't possible, just tape the streamers on the index finger of each child's hand.) Explain to the children that the colors of their streamers represent Mexico and Our Lady of Guadalupe.

Explain that you will be processing around the room (and if possible, outside and around the building), as you pray the prayer over and over. Invite the children to hold the streamers high and sway them from side to side as they process. End your procession at your "shrine" of Our Lady of Guadalupe (your prayer table). There invite children to call out persons, places, and things they want to pray for. Encourage them to be universal with their prayers, and then conclude with one of their favorite hymns to Our Lady.

✾ Saint Lucy

Teacher Info

St. Lucy was from the country of Sicily and died as a martyr in the year 304 during the persecution of Emperor Diocletian. We don't know much about her except that from earliest times, people have prayed to her for healing eye problems.

Her feast day is December 13, and on that day the church prays: "Lord, give us courage through the prayers of St. Lucy. As we celebrate her entrance into eternal glory, we ask to share her happiness in the life to come."

For the activity on this page, have available two strips of paper for each child (11"x14").

The aim of this activity is twofold: 1) to honor St. Lucy, a woman who gave her life for Jesus, and 2) to become more conscious of God's great gift of sight.

Begin by telling the children that St. Lucy is one of the saints we honor during Advent. Then give each child two strips of paper. With the first one have them cut out eyeglasses. First, have them draw two circles with a connecting bridge and the ear pieces. Then have them cut out the whole thing, including the inside of the circles. (NOTE: With younger children you will probably have to do this with them step-by-step or cut the glasses out yourself ahead of time.)

Now, tell the children that, since St. Lucy is patroness of people with eye problems, we want to celebrate this feast day by thanking God for our wonderful gift of sight and praying for those with eye problems.

Ask them to do the following:

1) Put their new glasses on.

2) Close their eyes.

3) Open their eyes, look at one thing, and write it down on their paper.

4) Do this five more times, then put their pencils down and take the glasses off.

Now, tell the children that you are going to thank God for all the things that we can see with our wonderful eyes. Ask for volunteers to fill in the blank with the five things they have listed on their paper as you read this prayer: "For letting me see _____." Then have the entire class respond, "Thank you, God."

When everyone who wishes to do so has shared his or her list, ask the children to place their hands gently on their eyes, while you pray with hand outstretched in their direction:

Good and gentle Creator of our wonderful eyes, / thank you for the gift of sight. / Amen! / St. Lucy, / pray for all persons / who have eye problems. / Amen!

Helpful Hint

If you have blind or otherwise visually challenged children in your class, invite them to tell the other children what they "see"—colors, shapes, lights—and together thank God for that, letting them know that God, in infinite love, gifts them in special ways. Your respectful way of handling this will make visually challenged children feel like VIPs and raise the awareness of the sighted.

4 Christmas Eve

Teacher Info

Though you don't have class on Christmas Eve, you can be teaching the children in your class indirectly that day. It's all a matter of pre-preparation. You will already have done much preparation for Christmas during Advent, but you can still be a big help to families by giving the children a few activities to use at home. On this page you will find several simple suggestions.

1) On your last class before Christmas holidays begin, have the children make an envelope by folding a piece of 8"x11" poster paper (red, green, or white) in half and decorating it. Then have them print on the envelope, "My Christmas Eve Gifts for Jesus." Give them pieces of scrap paper and have them fold these into "gifts." Ask them to think of things they can do (or avoid doing) to make their families happy on Christmas Eve, and, thus, to prepare to commemorate Jesus' birthday. Have them draw some kind of code on the gifts, so that only God and they will know what the gifts are, and place these gifts in their envelopes.

Have them take these envelopes home and, on Christmas Eve, take out the gifts to recall what they will be doing for their families during the Christmas holidays. Remind them that what they do for their families, they are doing for Jesus.

2) This season seems to be made for angels. Give the children a short lesson on how to make an angel. Draw a triangle, put a circle on top and two little flaps on the side for wings, and you have an angel! Have the children cut out eight or ten of these (about 4" high) and take them home in an envelope to give to parents or caregivers.

Send a short note home explaining that for each good thing this child does, the parent or caregiver should hang one of the little angels—with the child's name on it—on the Christmas tree. These are to be gifts for both Jesus and the child's family. (NOTE: This activity could easily be expanded to a family activity, thus producing inexpensive decorations for the tree.)

3) Have the children make little figures like paper dolls, representing each person in their families, including the extended family. Then, on Christmas Eve, the children can do kind deeds for family members. After the act is done, the child can put the "doll" representing the person for whom the act was done, at the créche or on the tree.

4) Give each child a prayer card to use at their family supper on Christmas Eve. You can write an original prayer, or use this (adapted) one from the Christmas Midnight Mass: "God, our Father, you make this holy night radiant with the splendor of Jesus Christ, our light. We welcome him as Lord, the true light of the world. Bless this meal we are about to share and bless us, too. Amen."

The basic idea behind these simple activities is to encourage children to think of others, and to focus on "the reason for the season."

5 Christmas Day

Teacher Info

Naturally, you won't be teaching on Christmas Day! I take that back—yes, you will be teaching on Christmas Day. Hopefully, what has happened in your class during Advent in preparation for Christmas will be going into action in the homes of the children whose lives you have touched.

You probably have enough Christmas projects already. Just in case, though, here are a few more. (Remember that the Christmas season extends beyond Christmas Day!)

1) Most of you probably give the children in your class little gifts to take home as you bid them good-bye for the Christmas holidays—a candy cane, a little Christmas stocking, a red pencil with a green bow on it. Well, let me suggest a little addition: a booklet. Write an original "Prayer Before Meals for Christmas" and a "Prayer After Meals for Christmas." Print or type these on a 4"x5 1/2" piece of paper, the Prayer Before Meals on the left, the Prayer After Meals on the right. Copy these on the copier and then fold the papers in half and staple them into a red or green cover made of half a sheet of 8"x11" poster paper. Place a Christmas sticker on the front (or a big shiny star) and you have your gift booklets. Or, if you have time, take your used Christmas cards and cut scenes from them to paste on the covers of your booklets. Get a roll of Christmas ribbon to tie around the booklets, and you will have an attractive gift indeed. Suggest that the children use these prayers at meals with their families on Christmas Day and throughout the Christmas season.

2) Have the children decorate large, brown grocery bags and keep them in a safe and secret place at home until Christmas Day. Then, after the family has unwrapped gifts and left paper everywhere, the children can bring out the bag, show it off, and announce that, as a special Christmas service, they will collect all the trash in this bag and put it in the trash bin. This will be a welcome surprise to tired parents or caregivers.

3) This suggestion has to do with recycling. Suggest that the children "rescue" any used Christmas paper that has designs on it. Have them cut out the designs and glue them to pieces of plain note paper. These can be used as thank-you notes to send to family and friends from afar, and also to family members who put up the tree and crèche, decorated the house, and did cooking and cleaning.

4) Challenge the children to observe the twelve days of Christmas (from Christmas Day to January 6) by doing something special for a family member each day (thus doing something special for Jesus!)

Did You Know?
The church is not finished with Christmas on December 25. Christmas songs continue to be sung until the feast of the Epiphany. The feast of the Holy Family is celebrated on the Sunday between Christmas and New Year's. December 26 commemorates the first martyr, Stephen; on December 27, the church remembers the evangelist St. John; and on December 28, it observes the feast of the Holy Innocents. January 1, New Year's Day, is the octave of Christmas. Then there is Epiphany, which in ancient times was a major Christmas celebration, and finally, the feast of the Baptism of the Lord closes out the season.

6 Saint Stephen

Teacher Info

St. Stephen was chosen by the apostles as one of the first seven deacons of the church. We know that there are two kinds of deacons: 1) those who are deacons on the way to being ordained priests, and 2) those who are permanent deacons. The permanent deacons, who can be married or single, serve the people of God in various ways: They can baptize and officiate at weddings, wakes, and funerals; they can give homilies and distribute communion.

Deacons minister in prisons, hospitals, and nursing homes. They also teach and help troubled young people and the poor, and serve in other ways in the church.

We are told that St. Stephen was commissioned by the apostles to collect food for the poor. The story of his ministry and martyrdom is told in Acts 6:1–8:3. His feast day is December 26. (Note that the activity on this page and activities 7 and 8 can be used any time in December to anticipate these feast days.)

Begin this activity by sharing the story of Stephen, the first martyr and first deacon of the church. You might want to read the account in Acts, allowing children to take turns. After you have shared Stephen's story, list these highlights on the board (or on a large piece of paper using colored felt pens): Stephen was a follower of Jesus; he was the first Christian martyr; he was one of the first deacons; he spread the good news of the gospel; he served the church by feeding the poor.

Now announce: "Let's make believe that we are members of the St. Stephen Fan Club. We want to share all we can about him, because we admire him so much. Our goal is to tell as many people as possible about him: our families, our neighbors, our friends—everyone."

Give the children pieces of paper and have them write the five highlights of Stephen's life. Then offer them this tip about sharing this information with others (lest they get carried away): Courtesy is an essential in spreading the good news; and our aim is to share, not to knock people over with, our superior knowledge!

Try role-playing how you might share information about Stephen. (You take the role of the child and ask a child to take the role of "Mrs. McDonald.")

Teacher: "Say, Mrs. McDonald, do you know about St. Stephen?"

Mrs. McDonald: "Er…well, I've heard about him, but, no, I can't say I know much about him.

Teacher (showing your list): "I didn't know much about him either until lately. But I found him so interesting that I'd like to share information with you."

Mrs. McDonald: "OK!"

Teacher (after showing the list): "My teacher said that we can do many of the things Stephen did in our lives right now (point to the items). We can be followers of Jesus; we can spread the good news; and we can help the poor."

Mrs. McDonald: "Thank you so much for sharing this."

Now reverse the roles and you be the adult. At the end of this activity, you might want to commission the children in this way. Hold your right hand in blessing toward them as you pray this "Prayer after Communion" from the Mass of St. Stephen:

"Lord, we thank you for the many signs of your love for us. Save us by the birth of your Son and give us joy in honoring St. Stephen, the martyr." Then add: "May you spread the word about Stephen so that others can imitate his faith and love for Jesus. Amen."

7 Saint John the Evangelist

Teacher Info

Lately, we are hearing a great deal about evangelization, which means proclaiming the gospel message to those who do not yet know or have not yet received it, and explaining it more fully for those who have received it.

In a nutshell, evangelization concerns us Christians in this way: We are all called to evangelize, which is the primary mission of the church. We have an obligation to evangelize those who have never heard the good news and those who could stand a little updating.

The Catechism of the Catholic Church doesn't use the term "evangelization," but covers the same ground under the heading "Mission" (849-856). St. John the Evangelist, along with Matthew, Mark, and Luke, gave us the four gospels—the good news of salvation, which is the object of evangelization. Incidentally, the word gospel comes from the Anglo-Saxon god-spell and the Greek evangelion, which mean "good news."

For this activity, give each child an envelope or a "pocket" made by folding a paper in half and stapling the ends, plus a piece of paper. Put the names of all the children (yours, too) in a box or a bag , and have each child pick a name. (They should write the name they picked on the front of the envelope.) Then direct them to look for a passage in their bibles that is "good news" to them, which they can share with the person whose name is on the envelope.

On the piece of paper have the children write out their good news messages and put them in the envelopes. On the back of the envelope, each child should write his or her own name. When everyone is ready, call the children forward one by one to proclaim their messages. As they do so, they should look in the direction of the person whose name they picked. If you feel that they might need help knowing how to proclaim the messages in their envelopes, offer examples like these:

"I pass on to you, (person's name), the good news that Jesus multiplied the loaves to show us how to care for one another (John 6:1–15)."

"I pass on to you, (person's name), the good news that Jesus calmed the sea and he can calm the troubles in our lives (Luke 8:22–25)."

After sharing the message, they should "deliver" the envelope. When all have had a turn, tell the children the beauty of what they have done: They have passed on the good news of Jesus Christ.

Conclude by moving to your prayer space and, as children hold their good news envelopes, have them pray along in their hearts as you pray aloud:

Holy Spirit, God, / thank you for helping us / to pass on the good news of Jesus Christ / to one another. / Please help us to learn all we can, / so that some day / we may be able to share the gospel / with people who have never heard it. / Amen.

Feast of the Holy Innocents

The story of the Holy Innocents is best told by St. Matthew himself. I usually start the reading at Matthew 2:1 with the visit of the kings. That way, the tragedy is arrived at with the proper preparation, introduced by the flight into Egypt. After the reading, go to the board and write: "Why?" Under it, write: greed, selfishness, abuse of power.

You might want to share the following definitions: Greed is wanting and taking more than we need. Selfishness is thinking only of our own needs and ignoring those of others. Abuse of power is taking away the rights of others in order to remain in charge.

Herod was guilty of these three sins. He was afraid that the infant Jesus would grow up and take his kingdom from him.

Explain that this story should inspire us to examine our behavior. Are we ever greedy or selfish? Do we ever abuse our power? Share these practical examples.

• If you're first in line in the cafeteria and you take all the chips and don't leave any for anyone else, that's being greedy.

• If you stand at the pencil sharpener and sharpen eight pencils and the others don't have any time left to sharpen theirs, that's selfish.

•If you are the captain of a team, you have the power to choose the players. You would be abusing your power if you chose only your friends.

Invite comments and questions and then say: "Like Herod, we can all be greedy and selfish; we can all abuse power. But, with the help of Jesus, we can turn these habits around. When we feel greedy, we can ask Jesus to help us to share, and he will. When we feel selfish, we can ask Jesus to help us to think of others first, and he will. When we feel like abusing power, we can ask Jesus to help us to be fair and just, and he will."

If you have time, have the children compose a short prayer telling Jesus they are sorry for the times they have been greedy or selfish, and for the times they have abused power. Have them ask Jesus for help not to be that way.

Feast of the Holy Family

Teacher Info

Teacher Info

The family is the most important unit in the world. That must be the reason that the new Catechism of the Catholic Church spends so much space and effort on the family.

The best background preparation for the Feast of the Holy Family (observed on the first Sunday after Christmas), would be for you to study the Catechism sections on the family (2197 to 2233).

The activity on this page can be done shortly after classes resume or anytime in January. You will need two sentence strips or posters, with these phrases written on them: gives glory to God, and gives service to others. You will also need seventeen index cards on which are printed the following qualities (all taken from the Catechism): give up my own way for others, peace, joy, forgiveness, honor for everyone in the family, sharing, cooperation, daily prayer, reading of God's word, care of the very young, care of the elderly, care of the handicapped, security—feeling safe, authority of parents, obedience of children, good use of freedom, visiting poor or sad relatives.

To begin, tell the children that on the Sunday after Christmas the church celebrates the feast of the Holy Family. Ask: "What do you think makes a family holy?" The *Catechism of the Catholic Church* says that a family that is holy does two things (dramatically hold up your two sentence strips): gives glory to God and gives service to others (2013).

Put the sentence strips down quickly and challenge: "Who can repeat the two things without looking?" (It could be that none of them will be able to. If that is the case, hold up the cards again, long enough for them to see the information. By that time, they will all know it.)

Now give each child a piece of paper and invite them to go shopping for qualities they would like their families to have. Spread the index cards you prepared beforehand all around the room. Have children "shop," move at random from card to card, and write down the numbers of the qualities they want to "buy." Give them sufficient time for this.

When the shopping is done, put all the cards on the board, and suggest that they discuss these qualities at home with their families.

To conclude this activity, have all the children hold their "shopping lists" in praying hands, while they repeat after you:

Jesus, Mary, and Joseph, / Holy Family, / please help our families to be holy, too. / Help us to give glory to God / and service to others. / Help us to get the things / that are on our shopping lists. / We ask this in the holy name of Jesus. / Amen.

Helpful Hint

Whenever you want children to memorize certain facts, try this fun little drill. First show the items you want memorized (not too many at a time) and then hide the items and challenge anyone to name them. If most can't, show the items again, and then ask for answers. Most will do better this time. Another way to do this is to call on a volunteer to face the back of the room and repeat the items. Then have another face the prayer corner, another face the cabinet, and each time repeat the items. Then, stop the game suddenly and say: "Now, everyone whisper it to me!" (After all the excitement of the drill, if you ask them to answer in a normal voice, the volume will be too high, so ask them to whisper.) By then, the items you want them to remember will stay in their heads a long time.

10 New Year's Eve

Teacher Info

On New Year's Eve in the classrooms of the (western) world, not a creature will be stirring, not even a mouse! Then why a project for New Year's Eve? In my experience, most dedicated teachers and catechists can find ways to slip prayer into all kinds of unlikely events. In fact, the more unlikely the better, because Jesus is present in every situation of our lives.

So, since children will not be coming to class on New Year's Eve, you can go to them through the "pre-fab" activity on this page. For it you will need five 2"x8" paper strips and a business envelope for each child.

Before the Christmas break, tell the children that you want to prepare with them a New Year's Eve prayer activity that they can do with their families.

Give each child five paper strips. Explain that on one side of each strip they will be writing a word or a phrase that describes the past year, plus the short prayer "Thank you, Jesus." On the other side they will write a word or phrase that describes the kind of new year they want to have, plus the short prayer "Please, Jesus." Before they write anything, you might offer some suggested words and phrases.

For the past year, for example, you might suggest: birthday party, family trip, good grades, new friends, baseball, swimming, and books. For the coming year, you might suggest: happiness, good health, good friends, trips, and games. In both cases, invite children to add words or phrases.

Now, ask the children to choose words from your list or think of their own and write one word or phrase on each of their five strips that describes the past year, plus the prayer "Thank you, Jesus." Then have them flip the papers over and choose the five things they would like to happen in the coming year, plus the prayer "Please, Jesus."

Then, ask the children to put the five strips together, the past-year side up, and help them staple the strips on the left to form a booklet. Have them place these booklets in their envelopes.

Suggest that they take the booklets home and put them in a safe place until New Year's Eve, when they will use them for a mini end-of-the-year family prayer service. It might be wise to send a note home to parents explaining that their children have made these booklets and suggest ways to use them. For example, the service can begin with a short prayer like: "Dear God, thank you for the past year that we were able to be together as a family. Watch over us as we look forward to a new year of life together." Then the child can call out the words he or she has written and each family member can add a personal contribution to it, after which the family prays either "Thank you, Jesus" or "Please, Jesus" together.

On New Year's Eve, as you drop off to sleep, you can be consoled knowing that the children in your class very likely prayed with their families because of something you did!

JANUARY

Ideas & Activities

1. Solemnity of Mary
2. Epiphany
3. Baptism of Jesus
4. "Make Your Dreams Come True" Day
5. Saint Ita (Ida)
6. Martin Luther King
7. The Conversion of St. Paul
8. Saint Angela Merici
9. Saint Thomas Aquinas
10. The Season of Winter

✠ Solemnity of Mary

Teacher Info

On January 1 the church observes the Solemnity of Mary, mother of God. What a beautiful way to begin a new year, with Mary, our mother, opening the door for us, as it were, carrying in her arms the savior of the world. The activity on this page is intended to help children begin this new year in Mary's company. It can be done any time in January. If possible have available a statue or a picture of Mary.

Draw a huge pie shape (cut into wedges) on the board or on a poster. Then say: "It would be somewhat difficult to eat this whole pie all at once, but it's easy to enjoy it a piece at a time. In the same way, we might have a problem handling a whole year, but one day at a time isn't bad!"

Give out large pieces of paper and direct the children to draw as big a circle as they can. Explain that the circle will be a symbol of one month of the coming year. Then direct them to draw a line in the middle to indicate a half and then another line to indicate fourths (each of the four parts represents one of the four weeks in a month). Finally, ask them to write in thirty-one numbers, in any order, all over the pie.

Now invite them to think of one thing they can do every day of the coming month to honor Mary, our mother. For example: 1) do one act of kindness every day; 2) give a compliment to someone; 3) say a Hail Mary for parents or caregivers daily; 4) try to read a little section of the bible every day; 5) do at least one thing around the house to help—every day.

Have the children write their choice at the bottom of their paper. Tell them that the pie will help them to remember what they promised and they can keep a record of how they are doing by circling one of the numbers each day that they remember their promise.

For your closing prayer, have the children form a circle, each holding their pie. If you have a statue or picture of Mary, place it in the center of the circle. Then have the children sing a favorite hymn to Our Lady or pray a Hail Mary.

If you think of it, you might remind the children at the end of January that it's time to make a "pie" for February, and so on throughout the year.

Helpful Hint

Explain to children that Mary always points the way to her son, Jesus. When we pray to her or honor her in any way, we are asking that she guide our steps toward Jesus. The church recognizes that Jesus is the center and focal point of our faith. Consider this Prayer after Communion, which is said at Mass on January 1: "Father, as we proclaim the Virgin Mary to be the mother of Christ and the mother of the Church, may our communion with her son bring us to salvation. We ask this through Christ Our Lord. Amen."

2 The Feast of Epiphany

Teacher Info

Did you know that the feast of Epiphany (observed on January 6 or on the Sunday between January 2 and 8) was being celebrated in the church even before the feast of Christmas? Well, it's a fact! That tells us how important this feast is. Epiphany means manifestation and the feast is so named because the gospel of the day (Matthew 2:1–12) tells us about the Magi, who went looking for Jesus and were rewarded by a manifestation of him.

The activity on this page centers on looking for Jesus everywhere—and, of course, on finding him! You may want to schedule it for your first class in January. You will need tape, cut-out stars, one for each participant, plus rulers, pencils, or twigs to tape the stars to.

Begin your celebration by announcing to all present that this is a celebration of Epiphany, the manifestation of Jesus to the world; and it will commemorate the search of the three kings for Jesus. Say: "As they searched for Jesus, so will we. As the three kings were led by a star, so will we be…in a way."

Have some helpers assist you in giving out the stars and whatever you are using to tape them to. Help each person tape on the stars. The result will look something like a wand. Then have everyone hold up the stars as you pray: "Jesus, Savior, today we celebrate your Epiphany and, as the three kings sought you, we will also search for you."

Explain to the children that Jesus promised to be with us always through the Holy Spirit. Though he is with us, we may not be aware of his presence. The purpose of our search is really to open our eyes and hearts to this presence. Now, suggest that all take a moment of silence to decide where they might search for Jesus.

You might want to make a few suggestions: I will look for Jesus in my parents, in the tabernacle, in the eucharist (or other sacraments), on the bus, at the mall, in a person I dislike, on TV, in my best friend, in the elderly and the sick, in nature.

Now, ask your class to move in procession to your prayer table. One by one have each child announce: "I will look for Jesus (name of place)." After each announcement, all should respond: "May you find Jesus where you search for him. Amen. Alleluia!"

After the celebration, you might suggest that everyone take the stars home and post them in a prominent place as a reminder to look for Jesus everywhere, in everyone, and in everything.

Helpful Hint

Try to be as creative as possible with your class processions. For most of us, the distance to the prayer table in our teaching space is short, so we have to devise ways to make our journey there a real procession. Background music is a plus. Play it as you lead children around the room several times. Another option is to teach children a chant that they can recite as they process. For example, when celebrating Epiphany, as above, have children chant: "Where are you, Jesus? Open our hearts to you always." If your group is able to sing, you can teach them songs for use during processions. "We Three Kings" is a natural choice for Epiphany. Whenever possible, move your processions down the hall and outside and invite children to carry objects they have made or been given, such as the stars in this activity.

☀ *Baptism of Jesus*

Begin with this announcement: "Today, we are going to look at the baptism of Jesus, which we usually celebrate on the Sunday after Epiphany. (Sometimes it is celebrated the Monday after Epiphany.) This feast day closes the Christmas season, and you can read about what it celebrates in your bibles in Matthew 3:13–17. Let's read it together now!" Afterward, pause for a moment of silent respect for the Word of God. Go to the board and write these three words: call, work (mission), acceptance (saying yes).

Then say, "It was at his baptism that Jesus received the call and learned what his life work was to be. It was at this time also that he accepted it. At our baptism we too were called to do our lifetime work, and day by day to accept it."

Then invite the class to play charades. Tell the children that God calls us every day to do something for others and every day we can say yes or no. Explain that everyone will get a chance to act out one thing God is calling him or her to do. Begin yourself by going to the front of the room, facing the children and asking, "What is God calling me to do right now?" Pick up a book and use gestures to indicate that you are teaching. Most likely someone will guess this. (If you think it will help, have slips of paper available on which some items are written, for example, study hard, sing a song, help a friend, do the dishes, take out the trash, clean the chalkboard, help the teacher, etc.) Continue until every child has had a turn to act out something God wants them to do.

Then call three children up to hold cards that read: 1) Call; 2) Work; and 3) Yes and No (two cards). Stand behind child #1 and demonstrate the next part of this activity. Say, "God calls me!" Then move behind child #2 and say, "to teach the good news to this class!" Move to child #3 and say, "Now, at this point, I can accept or not. I accept!" Child #3 drops the No card and leaves the Yes card up.

Now, have each child go through the three steps, using the "work" each used in the charades. After all have had a turn, move to your prayer table and invite the children to pray spontaneous prayers, asking for God's help to do the work they are called to do.

Teacher Info

The feast of the baptism of Jesus closes the Christmas season. It is closely related to Epiphany, in that both feasts focus on the manifestation of Jesus as Messiah. Both mark beginnings in the life of Jesus: Epiphany, the beginning of his life; baptism, the beginning of his public life.

In trying to present this feast to children, I've narrowed it down to three interconnected ideas which I think they can grasp:

1. The Call—God's voice is heard.

2. The Work (mission)—Jesus is revealed as Messiah, a person for others.

3. Acceptance—Jesus accepts his mission.

(For further background for yourself, I suggest: Isaiah 42:1–4,6–7; Acts 10:34–38; Mark 1:6b–11. I also recommend the Catechism of the Catholic Church (438, 536-537, and 1223).

4 "Make Your Dreams Come True" Day

Begin by asking the children if they could be anywhere they wanted to be, doing anything they wanted to do, where would they be, and what would they be doing? If they could be whatever kind of person they wanted to be, what kind of person would they be?

You can take a turn first by saying something like this: "If I could be where I wanted to be and be doing what I wanted to do, I'd be sitting high up in the Alps, in Bavaria, yodeling and enjoying the gorgeous scenery in the valleys below! And the kind of person I'd be is the kindest person in the world!"

Then ask for volunteers to share their "dreams" with the class. (The first time I tried this, I was so disappointed. I felt like a catechetical failure because none of the children said they wanted to be saints or angels or martyrs—or even good people! But then I remembered that at their age I hadn't wanted to be those things either!)

When all have had a turn to name their "dreams," give out the papers and have them draw some aspect of their "dreams." When the drawings are completed, invite the children to come forward one by one to share what they have drawn. That done, ask these questions: "Can all these dreams come true?" (Response: "No!") "Are there dreams that can come true?" (Response: "Yes!") "If we want our dreams to come true, what are some things we have to do?"

Maybe, just maybe, someone will say, "pray" or "ask God for help," but it's unlikely. You will probably have to lead them to that. One way to begin is to teach them this brief ditty:

It's good to dream and aim up high, / It's good to work and plan and pray, / Because we know those things can help / To make our dreams come true some day.

For your closing prayer, process to your prayer corner and have each child place his or her "dream" on the table there. Then, invite everyone to extend their arms toward the prayer table and repeat after you:

Great and beautiful God / it is you who have placed all our dreams / in our minds and hearts. / Please help us to do all that needs to be done / to make our dreams come true / not only our own dreams / but those of others, too. / Amen.

5 Saint Ita (Ida)

Begin this activity by briefly explaining who St. Ita is. Then ask the children, "If St. Ita lived so long ago, can her message have any meaning for us today?" Invite them to join you in figuring out the answer to this question.

Teacher Info

St. Ita (or Ida, as some call her) was, like Patrick, Brigid, and Brendan, an Irish saint. She was born in County Waterford around the end of the sixth century, in a wealthy family. Early in life, she decided to dedicate herself to God, and she founded a convent in Killeedy, County Limerick, where she remained all her life. She was so wise and holy that even bishops came to consult her. St. Ita was instrumental in directing two other saints, St. Brendan and St. Mochoemoc.

One day, St. Brendan asked her what three things pleased God most. Her answer was: 1) true faith in God with a pure heart, 2) a simple life with a religious spirit, and 3) a hand open in charity.

Brendan then asked what three things displeased God the most. Ita answered: 1) a scowling face, 2) hard-headedness in wrongdoing, and 3) putting one's trust in the power of money. St. Ita died in 570, and although she isn't well known, she has a terrific message for us. Her feast day is January 15.

On the board write:

What pleases God most:

true faith,

a simple life,

hands open to give.

What displeases God most:

a scowling face,

hard-headedness in wrong-doing,

trust in the power of money.

(It would be very effective if you have this information on a large, colorful poster, a long piece of newsprint, sentence strips, or cards.)

Divide the class into six groups and assign one item to each group. Ask the children to come up with ways they can do these things today, and have them offer examples. After a reasonable time, have each group report on the results of their discussions. After the last report, ask, "Do you think that this shows that St. Ita's message still fits our times?" End this activity with this prayer:

St. Ita / help us to have true faith / to live simple lives / and to open our hands for giving. / May we never have scowling faces / or be hard-headed. / May we put our trust in God alone. / Amen.

Did You Know?

If you are interested in an easy-to-read, easy-to-use lives of the saints, I recommend *Lives of the Saints*, revised by Rev. Hugo Hoever, S.O. Cist., Ph.D., Catholic Book Publishing Co., New York, NY, 1993 (1955). This book is full of stories about little-known saints. Also, Loyola University Press has a great resource called *Saints Kit*, which contains 189 saint cards that present the lives of more than 200 saints—along with a multitude of teaching ideas. The kit costs $39.95 and can be ordered by calling (800) 621-1008.

🌞 Martin Luther King Day

It would be a good idea to begin this class with a peace prayer, maybe a selection from the Mass for Peace and Justice, or the beautiful peace prayer of St. Francis of Assisi. Perhaps you might give each child a holy card with St. Francis' prayer on it, and suggest that the children pray it daily for peace in families and in countries all over the world.

Begin a discussion by asking children: "Do you think it's hard to be a peaceful person? Are there ways to settle problems peacefully without violence?" After allowing children to respond, explain that many people try to be people of peace. One who succeeded was Martin Luther King, Jr., who tried to imitate Jesus.

Then say, "Let's take Jesus first. He died rather than use the power he had to destroy his enemies. Martin Luther King, Jr. refused to fight back when people were violent and unjust toward him. Instead, he found nonviolent ways to deal with his enemies."

Next, on the board, make the following diagram: At the top, draw a rectangle, and print the word "conflict" in it. Below the rectangle, and connected to it by lines, draw two more rectangles. In the right one, print the word "peace," in the left one, print the word, "violence." Ask for a volunteer to describe a conflict. Then have the children give various ways they can arrive at a peaceful solution. Some examples might include: asking God for help, talking it over when possible, counting to ten, walking away for now, giving in if the matter is not important. The children will be able to add to the list. Then ask them to name some violent solutions to conflict. (I don't think they'll falter there.)

In order to keep this activity in the minds of the children, have them cut out circles and print "Peace IS Possible" on them. Then put a piece of tape on the backs of the circles and have the children wear them home.

7 The Conversion of Saint Paul

Teacher Info

The church commemorates the conversion of St. Paul on January 25. Paul, then known as Saul of Tarsus, was on his way to Damascus to persecute more Christians when he had an encounter with Jesus that he would never forget.

This story is one of the best illustrations of the doctrine of the Mystical Body of Christ, for Jesus says: Saul, Saul, why do you persecute me? Paul must have realized at that moment that what he did to the followers of Jesus, he did to Jesus as well.

Read Acts 9:1–22 with your class before you begin this activity. Then discuss what St. Paul was like before he came in contact with Jesus and after he met Jesus. If the children have trouble remembering, encourage them to look in their bibles. Then give them pieces of paper and ask them to fold them in half. At the top, they should print: "The Conversion of (their own names)." On the left side have them print "Before," and on the right side "After." Explain that all of us experience conversions from time to time, even children, for example:

- I used to stick gum under chairs; I don't do it anymore.
- I used to hit people; I don't anymore. • I used to be rude; I'm not anymore.
- I used to skip my prayers; I don't anymore.

Encourage them to think of examples that are true for them and then draw a picture of what they were like before and then after in the appropriate places on the paper. When they have finished their drawings, have them draw a cross between the two pictures in their favorite colors. Remind children that with Jesus' help all of us can change for the better.

Now, have the children carry their drawings to your prayer area and hold them between folded hands as they pray with you:

Jesus, when St. Paul met you / on the road to Damascus / his whole life was changed. / In our own lives / there are still things in us that need changing. (Invite the children to silently pause and think of what these are.) Please, Jesus / let us meet you in our lives / and thus change for the better. / Amen.

Helpful Hint

Paper is probably the most expensive item in our budgets and, Lord knows, we use tons of it. Well, when I taught in one of our poorer schools, we came up with ideas on how to hold our paper expenses down. I pass these ideas on to you.

1. Make friends with a company that uses or makes computer paper. They always have boxes of it that they can't use. Go after it!

2. Your copying machine makes all kinds of mistakes that humans don't claim. This results in reams of paper used on one side, but perfectly good on the other. What we did was put a box near the copying machine and put all ruined paper in it. Then for simple drawing or writing projects, we used the used paper. It works just as well and the children don't usually mind.

3. Ask parents if their workplaces throw out a lot of paper. If they do, ask them for it.

4. Publishing companies, grocery stores, department stores, paper mills, all kinds of places, have paper they don't need. Ask them to recycle it in your direction. By doing these things we save our trees and our budgets, too!

8 Saint Angela Merici

Teacher Info

Angela Merici was born in 1474 on the shores of Lake Gorda in Italy. When she was only fifteen years old, she joined the Third Order of St. Francis. From an early age, she felt called by God in a special way for service in the church. In 1535 she established a group of religious women, the Ursuline Sisters, who have passed on the good news through teaching right up to the present day.

She started schools for young girls, and, although there were already schools in monasteries, hers would be different. Instead of having the students come to the teachers, St. Angela sent her teaching Sisters out to the homes of the girls. Her idea, which is certainly still relevant to our world today, was that "disorders in society are the result of disorder in the family." St. Angela and her Sisters decided to see what they could do through their teaching to help families. Her feast day is January 27.

You might want to begin this activity by introducing St. Angela Merici, accenting the fact that she began the first teaching order in the church. Many children in your group may not have met a religious sister, so you will want to explain that fifty years ago, most Catholic schools in this country were staffed by religious sisters. Also explain that people don't have to be nuns to teach about God.

Then, tell the children that each one of them is, in some way, a teacher, and that whenever we share God's word with others, we are teaching them. Sharing God's word can be done in many ways, as the following activity demonstrates.

Ask the children to choose a favorite selection from the bible and think up a creative way to present it to the class. I suggest that you give them guidelines. For example, they can introduce their presentations by saying: "I'd like to tell you about this passage in God's word…."

They can then 1) read the passage to the class, 2) role-play the passage with the help of other children, 3) illustrate the passage and explain what they have drawn, 4) make up a poem about the passage, 5) stage a debate based on the passage.

Give children sufficient time to prepare these presentations and give them all the help they need so that this activity may be pleasant and joy-filled. It may get noisy, but that's okay as long as they are busy working on their presentations.

Once all the presentations are prepared, invite the children one by one to present them to the rest of the class. Be sure you lead the others in applause and praise.

For your closing prayer, have children gather around your prayer space for this closing prayer.

Teacher: For the gift of your good news, dear God…

Children: Thank you, God, thank you!

Teacher: For the gift of the beautiful messages we received today…

Children: Thank you, God, thank you!

Teacher: For the help you give us to share the good news with family and friends…

Children: Thank you, God, thank you. Amen!

Saint Thomas Aquinas

Teacher Info

St. Thomas Aquinas is a special saint for catechists, having been named patron of Catholic education in 1880. And that's not all! In 1567 he was named a doctor of the church. What does it mean to be a doctor of the church? These were men and women writers of great learning and sanctity, whose writings were immensely valuable to the whole church. (For detailed information on the men and women doctors of the church, see The Catholic Almanac, Our Sunday Visitor, 200 Noll Plaza, Huntington, IN 46750. The church celebrates Thomas Aquinas' feast day on January 28.

Introduce this activity this way: "Today we are going to get acquainted with the patron saint of Catholic education, St. Thomas Aquinas. Thomas was a doctor of the church. That means that he was two great things. I'm going to see if you can guess what these two things are."

Write "S" on the board. Then say: "I have a riddle for you that will help you guess the two great qualities that St. Thomas Aquinas had. Both words begin with 'S'; both words have three letters between the beginning and ending letters, and both words end in 'T.'" (Your riddle should look like this: S _ _ _ T.) "I'll even give you a clue: The words are synonyms for holy and intelligent." (The children will likely guess "saint" and "smart.") Explain that there were both men and women doctors of the church, who lived and wrote for the good of the church. Though most of the children in your class will never be doctors of the church, they can strive to be both saints and smart!

Now give the children large pieces of paper and ask them to write their names at the top and to draw two lines, one under their first name and the other after their surname. At the end of the first line they should draw a box and write the word "saint" in it. At the end of the second line they should draw a box and write the word "smart" in it. Direct the children to think of things they can do or are already doing that would qualify them as "saints" and as "smart." List some of these on the board to get the children started, but challenge them to think up original words.

Under "saints" you might list: I love Jesus; I read the bible and try to be like Jesus; I love and obey my parents and teachers; I make friends with people nobody likes; I tell the truth; I do my work; I serve the poor.

Under "smart" you might have things like: I try to study hard at school and in religion class; I choose my friends carefully; I don't break other people's stuff; I ask elderly friends and neighbors for advice.

If you're lucky, some child may come up with the conclusion that being a saint and being smart have a lot in common. Now, have children fill in their papers, and if they want to include drawings, that's fine, too. When the papers are finished, carry them in procession to your prayer space, and invite children to say spontaneous prayers of thanks for the gifts of holiness and intelligence they already possess.

10 The Season of Winter

Teacher Info

With its ice, snow, and cold, January is the epitome of winter in many parts of North America. Winter can be a pain, but it can also be a blessing. Winter brings quiet. Everything is dormant, or so it seems. In earlier times this was more apparent, but now with antifreeze and plowed streets, people can keep moving as usual. But there is still something "quiet" about winter.

Quiet! Who needs it? We all do! Everything in nature seems to suggest that all of creation needs it: waking, sleeping; activity, rest; day, night; growing, lying fallow. So what does that have to do with us catechists? Plenty!

We have before us a roomful of children who seem to have non-stop motors. They are active and noisy! But, we remember that Jesus went up to the mountain to a quiet place to pray. He invited his followers to "come aside" and rest.

We catechists can do those we teach a great service if we give them the quiet time for reflection and prayer that is so much needed in their hectic young lives. Thus the activity on this page invites them to experience quiet.

Begin by explaining that our world is full of noise and that we are going to try to get away from it for a while. Explain that Jesus valued quiet, and he would go up into the hills and spend quiet time alone, praying. He invited his followers to "come aside and rest a while." Encourage the children to discuss their quiet times, if they have them, and whether or not they have a "quiet place."

Then have them spread out around the room, finding a comfortable place. Tell them that since it is not possible to go to our favorite quiet places right now, we can use our imaginations to go there. Dim the lights or turn them off, and invite the children to imagine themselves in their special quiet place. (Allow sufficient time for this and then turn the lights back on, and have everyone return to their places.) Invite the children to take turns saying where they were and then saying a brief spontaneous prayer of thanks for that place. For example: I went to my favorite spot under the bushes in our backyard and I thank God for the sounds of birds and my dog who came over to see what I was doing!

After you have shared all the quiet places, move to your prayer space. You've guessed it, the prayer for this activity should be a silent one. Invite the children to sit on the floor and talk to God about anything they want to talk about. After two minutes of so, end the experience by praying "Thank you, God," together (say it at least five times, a little louder each time).

Helpful Hint

An alternate to this activity is to introduce Jesus into the experience. For example, you might lead the children in this way: "Close your eyes and slowly count to ten backwards (pause). When you reach 'one,' picture yourself on a beautiful beach (pause). As you walk along, hearing the waves and smelling the salty air, you see someone coming toward you. No one else is on the beach, but you are not afraid. As the person gets closer, you realize that it is Jesus. He greets you by name and says that he has been thinking about you. You feel very happy and peaceful. Walk along with Jesus now and tell him whatever is on your mind (longer pause). When Jesus says goodbye, you walk back down the beach thinking about how good it felt to talk to him. Now slowly count to ten and when you reach 'ten' open your eyes."

FEBRUARY

SUN	MON	TUES	WED	THURS	FRI	SAT

Ideas & Activities

1. Candlemas Day

2. Saint Blaise

3. Norman Rockwell's Birthday

4. Four Holy Women

5. Thomas Edison Day

6. Valentine's Day

7. Shrove Tuesday

8. Ash Wednesday

9. Lent

10. More for Lent

Candlemas Day

Teacher Info

The Feast of the Presentation (February 2) was celebrated as early as the fifth century. In Rome it was observed with a penitential flavor and in France it was observed with solemn blessings and processions of candles and was popularly called "Candlemas."

The liturgy of the Feast of the Presentation is very lovely, and I recommend that you read and meditate on its prayers and readings before doing the activity on this page. The liturgy begins with a clarion call: "God will come with mighty power and give light to the eyes of all who serve Him, Alleluia!"

Then there is the blessing of the candles and a procession into the church. The Mass has three beautiful readings, plus Psalm 24, which glorifies the King of Glory. This is followed by the preface, which ends: "Our hearts are joyful for we have seen our salvation!"

For this activity you will need pieces of 8"x11" paper as well as 2"x2" yellow pieces. If possible, have a picture of Jesus for your prayer table. And finally, make a sign that says "Light of the World."

Introduce the Feast of the Presentation by having the children pantomime (walk through) the Gospel for this day (the long form is from Luke 2:22–40). Here's how. Choose "characters" for all the people mentioned in the reading and then, as the reading is proclaimed (perhaps by several readers), the children should mime what is going on. Your first walk-through may be a little uneven, but that's okay, because the children won't be satisfied with doing it just once.

After the pantomime, explain that the church began to connect the blessing of candles with this feast, in order to honor Jesus as the Light of the World. Thus this day began to be called Candlemas Day.

Now, give each child a piece of paper (8"x11") to decorate as brightly as possible. Then have them roll their papers into "candles." (Be patient with those who never seem to get it right!)

Tape the "candles" (top, middle, and bottom). Then give each child a piece of the yellow paper, and ask them to draw a flame and cut it out. Glue, tape, or staple the flame inside the "candle," and you are ready for a Candlemas procession.

Process all around the room—between the desks, tables, boxes, bookcases—with "candles" held high, singing "This Little Light of Mine." Feel free to improvise with this song. For example, add lines like "Jesus is my Light… (I'm gonna let him shine), In my home and school… In my head and heart…" When you arrive at your prayer corner, lead children in the following prayer:

> **Teacher:** Jesus, you are the Light of the World…
>
> **Children:** Shine on us always.
>
> **Teacher:** Jesus, you are the light of our lives.
>
> **Children:** Shine on us always.
>
> **Teacher:** Jesus, you are the light that guides our way.
>
> **Children:** Shine on us always. Amen.

Suggest that the children take their "candles" home and share the story of the Presentation and Candlemas Day with their families.

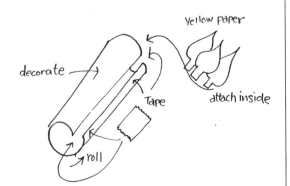

decorate / Tape / roll / Yellow paper / attach inside

Did You Know?

You can add a special decorative touch to prayer "candles" with tinsel. (You could use glitter, but it does get on your clothes, your shoes, the floor, the furniture—everything!) Cut small pieces of tinsel and tape them, front and back, onto the "flames" of all the candles. When children hold these up, they will literally shine.

22 Saint Blaise

Begin this activity by sharing information about St. Blaise and his blessing of throats. Then give the children a piece of paper and tell them that you each will be making a thank-you booklet to God for the gift of throats.

First, ask children to name as many things as possible that they can do with their throats: speak, sing, yell, cheer, pray, give compliments, teach, express love, share, ask for help.

Now, have them choose one of these abilities and draw a picture to go with it. Print the ability at the top of the paper and "Thank you, God!" at the bottom.

When all the papers are finished, staple them into a booklet. (While the children are working on their pictures, *you* might want to illustrate a cover.)

Choose a child for the honor of carrying this thank-you booklet to your prayer corner. To add to the solemnity, have all those who are lined up behind the booklet-bearer raise their hands (palms up) as they process. To extend your procession, have children chant the words "Thank you, God" over and over until they reach the prayer corner. Once there, place the booklet on your prayer table and have children pray after you:

Through the merits and intercession of St. Blaise / Bishop and Martyr / may God deliver us / from all diseases of the throat / and from every other evil / in the name of the Father / and of the Son / and of the Holy Spirit. / Amen.

Note: For occasions like this, you might want to invite a guest speaker to your class, an "expert" who can share information about blessings and rituals with the children. This might be your pastor, a DRE, or your parish deacon.

3 *Norman Rockwell's Birthday*

Teacher Info

Norman Rockwell was an American illustrator whose paintings were "homey" and at times very funny. He portrayed the best in American life, which is probably why his art appeals to so many. Rockwell's first paintings appeared in children's books and magazines. His birthday was February 3.

Why celebrate Norman Rockwell in religion class? Because talent is God-given, and children should know that all our talents can be used to enhance our Christian lives and to give joy to others.

By "talent" I mean a natural ability, a special and superior ability in some area. We have come to associate talent mainly with art, literature, and music, but in our hearts we know that God has given people talents of every kind. Thus the word talent can also apply to parenting, teaching, cleaning offices at night, officiating at a cash register, farming, canning tomatoes, flying a plane, or making soap—all of these tasks take "special, superior ability," or what we call "talent," to do well.

For this activity you will need 4"x4" pieces of paper, one for each child, a large piece of newsprint (or a cut-open grocery bag). At the top of the newsprint, write: "God Gave Talent," and at the bottom write, "To Everyone." Introduce Norman Rockwell by showing the children one of his paintings, or better yet a collection of them from the public library.

Invite the children to join you in celebrating his birthday by: 1) looking for God-given talent in unusual places, and 2) finding their own God-given talents. You may want to talk first about what "talent" means. Many children (and adults) use the word only in relation to artists, musicians, and the like. They may not equate "ordinary" tasks with talent. Give children examples of talented people from daily life, as in "Teacher Info."

Explain that talent is a natural ability, a special, superior ability in some area. The children will soon draw the conclusion that to do ordinary tasks really well does, indeed, take talent.

After this discussion, give the children 4"x4" pieces of paper and have them draw a picture of the most unusual talent they can think of (that most of us probably don't consider a talent). When all the "squares" are completed, have children come forward one by one to share what they have drawn. Once they share their drawings, have them tape them to the piece of newsprint to form a patchwork quilt. Assign two children to carry the quilt to your prayer space and there tape it to your prayer table. Invite the children to spend a moment in silence thinking of their own best talents. Close this activity by inviting them, one by one, to name one talent they admire, using this format:

Child: For the talent of _____.

All: Thank you, God.

Leave the quilt in your prayer space for a few weeks as a reminder that God gives us many and varied talents.

4 Four Holy Women

Teacher Info

February is a good month to celebrate holy women in the church because four holy women are honored this month: St. Agatha on February 5; St. Scholastica on February 10; St. Bernadette on February 11; and the greatest holy woman of all, Mary, our mother, also on February 11, under the title Our Lady of Lourdes.

Not much is known about St. Agatha, except that she came from a wealthy family in Sicily and suffered and died as a martyr for her faith in the year 251 A.D. Her name is mentioned in the first eucharistic prayer, indicating that she must have been influential in the early church.

St. Scholastica (480–547) was the twin sister of St. Benedict. She consecrated her life to God at an early age, and she later founded an order of Benedictine Sisters who followed the rule established by her brother Benedict (for his order of monks).

On February 11, we celebrate the feast of Our Lady of Lourdes. We know that Mary, under whatever title, is the greatest woman who ever lived. Why? Because she said "yes" to God, and thus fulfilled the purpose for which God had chosen her.

Bernadette Soubirous was a poor French peasant girl to whom Our Lady appeared in 1858 in Lourdes, France, giving her messages (a call to personal conversion, prayer, and chastity) that, if followed, would make our world a better place.

After you have told children about the four holy women whose feast days are observed in February, ask: "What do you think makes a person holy?" Encourage responses, but be sure to point out that holiness is not something "out of this world," but rather doing ordinary things as well as we can. Also stress that holiness involves loving God and loving others. You might want to use Mother Teresa of Calcutta as an example of a holy woman today, because the children are likely to be familiar with her and her work. Ask the children if they think Mother Teresa loves God and others. How does she show it?

Finally, ask: "Do you know any holy women personally?" Lead the children to the realization that there are many such holy women among us today who may not be extraordinary but who daily try to love God and others.

Now give the children pieces of cardboard and ask them to think of a holy woman they know personally. Have them draw and cut out, paper-doll style, a picture of the woman they have in mind.

When the "women" are all cut out, have the children color them and then mount them on a ruler, a pencil, or a stick. Then have each child introduce the person to the class by giving her name and telling how she shows love of God and others. (Don't forget to do one of these cutouts yourself!)

After all the introductions, have everyone hold up the "holy women," while you, or a designated child, prays:

Thank you, blessed God, / for giving us so many holy women / who love us and who love you, / and who show us how to love and serve others. / Amen.

5 Thomas Edison Day

Teacher Info

Thomas Edison was born in Milan, Ohio, on February 17, 1847. His father ran a grain and lumber business and his mother had been a teacher. She was way ahead of her time and believed that learning should be fun—an unusual belief at that time. She taught Thomas at home.

He often asked her questions she couldn't answer, however. When no one could give him answers, he experimented until he found them. He kept trying and trying, and we are told that he never became discouraged. He began inventing when he was very young, and eventually invented 1093 different things, not counting the improvements he made on many inventions of others. Because of Thomas Edison, we have the electric light, record players, voting machines, cement mixers, and thousands of other conveniences. We observe Thomas Edison Day on February 11.

What does Edison have to do with catechetics? A great deal if we share with children qualities he had that are essential to evangelization: 1) desire for knowledge, 2) willingness to find answers, 3) zeal, 4) persistence, 5) refusal to be discouraged.

Begin by sharing some of Thomas Edison's positive qualities, ones that children can use in their efforts to know Jesus better and to make him and his message known. Read the following and allow a moment of silence after each question.

1) Edison was curious and asked questions. Are we curious about Jesus and his word?

2) Edison did all he could to find answers to his questions. What are our questions about Jesus and what efforts do we make to find answers?

3) Edison didn't give up. Do we keep trying to find ways to know Jesus better and to share his gospel message?

4) Edison refused to let failure stop him. He just tried something else. Do we quit trying to make Jesus known, or do we try to find new ways to do it?

Now give the children pieces of paper and invite them to write a prayer to Jesus—in their own words—based on their answers to the four questions. These need not be elaborate; simple and from the heart is best. A sample might be: "Dear Jesus, help me to be more curious about you and your place in my life. I want to try harder. Amen."

When all the prayers are written, have the children carry them to the prayer table and place them in a basket or bowl. As you pray the following closing prayer, have one child hold up the container, as all repeat after you:

Jesus, we thank you for great people / like Thomas Edison. / Thank you for all that they have done / to make our lives easier. / Help us to use our gifts / to make you and your message known. / Amen.

🌸 Valentine's Day

Teacher Information

There are legends about two different St. Valentines—one who was martyred in Rome, and another one who was martyred in Interamna, 60 miles from Rome, around 269 A.D. At any rate, the remains of one St. Valentine were found in a catacomb in Rome.

Legend has it that one St. Valentine made friends with many children, and that when he was arrested and put into prison for being a Christian, the children missed him so much that they threw notes to him between the bars of the cell windows.

This may not have been the origin for sending valentines, but we do celebrate Valentine's Day on February 14, and children are fond of it and know that it is a day of love and caring.

Give each child three large hearts. Make these by tracing a heart from a stencil and copying it on a copier. Let the children cut out the hearts themselves. Then staple each set of hearts at the top to form a three-page tablet. On page one, ask the children to print "Jesus," on page two, "Others," and on page three, "Me." Now they can decorate the pages.

Explain that on Valentine's Day, we should try to think of Jesus first, then of others, and finally of ourselves, because Jesus is important, others are important, and we are important. Print the word "Jesus" on the board and ask, "What can we possibly give to Jesus?" Ask for suggestions (telling someone about him, praying for peace, going to Mass extra during the week, reading about him in scripture).

Next, print the word "Others" on the board and ask, "What can we do for others on Valentine's Day?" Answers might include sending a card to an unpopular child, visiting an elderly person, doing a loving deed for parents or siblings.

Now print the word "Me" on the board and say, "Jesus has told us to love others as we love ourselves, so we have to begin by loving ourselves, right? But how do we show love for ourselves?" Answers might include watching a favorite TV program, playing games you like, and praying for yourself, your friends, and your family.

When the discussion is over, have the children hold page one of the valentine booklet against their hearts, and tell Jesus silently what they want to give him this Valentine's Day.

Then, ask everyone to flip the page and hold page two against their hearts. Invite them to say a silent prayer for all those who will be receiving their valentines and for all those who will be lonely or left out on Valentine's Day.

When they flip to page three, they should say a prayer for themselves. Encourage children to take these booklets home as a reminder to love Jesus, others, and themselves.

7 Shrove Tuesday

Shrove Tuesday (alias Mardi Gras or Pancake Day) is a day of celebration before Ash Wednesday, which marks the beginning of Lent. Various countries call this celebration by different names. In Germany, it's called Fastnacht, in France and in the southern United States, it's called Mardi Gras, and in England, it's called Pancake Day! (That's right—Pancake Day!).

The word "shrove" comes from the practice of going to confession on the day before Ash Wednesday to be "shriven" of one's sins. Not a bad idea!

For the activity on this page, you will need three medium-sized waste cans and a bean bag. Borrow the cans from colleagues or your DRE. If you don't have a "bean bag," make one. Wad up some used paper, roll yarn around it, and you have a good throwing object that won't break windows or heads.

Space the three waste cans across the front of the room, below the chalkboard. On the board above each can, print these three words: giving, praying, fasting. Or you could make big colorful signs and tack them right on to the waste cans.

Begin by telling the children that Lent has three primary practices: giving, praying, and fasting. Now, choose a child (using your name cards) and have them stand approximately ten feet from the waste cans. (Mark this spot with masking tape.) Let the child try to make one of the "baskets" with the bean bag. If it lands in the "giving" can, the child should give an example of what could be "given" (not given up) during Lent, and so on for the other two categories. The game goes on until each child has had a turn.

What if a child misses? I mean, not all of us are throwing experts. Just let the child shoot until the bean bag goes in. After all, this isn't a competition; it's a learning experience. (Personally, I loathe competition! In my classes we did not compete with one another, not ever. The only competition I recognize, if it can be called that, is competing with oneself. I prefer to call this "aiming higher.")

When each child has had a turn (and you, too!) ask the children to close their eyes and tell what the three main practices of Lent are. After this fun drill, they probably will remember for the rest of their lives.

If possible, end this class with a sung prayer. One song that children really like is "I Have Decided to Follow Jesus" (#118 in the *Lead Me, Guide Me* hymnal.) It's one of those catchy tunes that once you sing it, it sticks with you all day.

If you can enlist the help of parents, serve the children donuts after this activity. They are easier to purchase and easier to eat in class than pancakes.

Helpful Hint

If possible, have a prize bucket in your class at all times that contains candies, stickers, or other small rewards for games—like the one on this page. My prize bucket was a tin can, the kind that government peanut butter comes in. But you can also use plastic popcorn buckets or other such containers. Small plastic toys, the Cracker Jack kind, make nice prizes and so do wrapped butterscotch and mint candies. Children love to get little prizes, but remember that they should not be rewarded for competing with one another, but for aiming higher themselves.

Ash Wednesday

For this activity you will need two twigs (or sticks) for each child, one longer than the other.

Begin by making a big happy face on the board. Put a large cross of "ashes" on its forehead. Then, under the face, print three words: sorry, friends, accept.

Tell the children that these are key words for Ash Wednesday, and that they explain the meaning of the ashes. When we are sorry, we have a chance during Lent to change our behavior for the better. Lent also gives us chances to become better friends with Jesus, and finally, it gives us opportunities to be patient and accept the hard things in our lives.

Now give each child one long and one short twig. Show them how to tie these together with yarn to make a cross, and, in case the children want to hang the crosses, just make a little yarn loop at the back of the cross. (Since some children will find this activity difficult, it would be great to have several parents present to help. In fact, it's always good to have such helpers around.)

After the crosses are tied together, give each child a small piece of paper and have them write the three "code words": sorry, friends, and accept. They can roll or fold the little papers and slip them in between the beams of their crosses.

Now invite the children to hold their crosses while moving to your prayer corner. Explain that you are going to ask them prayer questions that they can answer in their hearts in silence and talk to God about them. Allow sufficient time for this.

•This Lent, what can you do to show God that you are sorry for any wrong things you have done? (Pause)

•How can you develop your friendship with Jesus? (Pause)

• How can you show Jesus that you accept the hard things in your life—the things you cannot change? (Pause)

Conclude with this prayer:

Dear God, / you are slow to anger / and always ready to forgive. / Be with us / as we travel the road to Lent. / Lead us and guide us. / Amen.

The Season of Lent

Teacher Info

Lent is a time to examine our lives and see what needs changing in order for us to get closer to God and to others. It is a special time of prayer and forgiveness. It is a time to remember the price that Jesus paid for our salvation and to be grateful. Occurring as it does in springtime, Lent is also a time of new life and growth, in nature as well as in our lives.

In the activity for Ash Wednesday, we pinpointed three lenten practices: giving, praying, fasting. We will use these for this lenten activity as well. You will need at least two pieces of paper for each child and markers or crayons.

Helpful Hint

Offer children guidelines for setting up a personal prayer space at home, the center of which can be the cross they made for Ash Wednesday. Suggest that they fill a container (a paper cup, an old coffee cup, or a glass) with sand or dirt to serve as a stand for the cross. They can then get a doily or a small towel, table napkin, or scarf to place under it. You might want to give them a list of brief prayers they can say during Lent at this prayer corner. Also encourage them to pray spontaneously, using simple prayers like, "Be with me, Jesus," and "Thank you, God." Having their own space encourages children to pray often and from the heart.

Give each child a piece of paper and have them fold it in such a way that there is a little flap of about one inch at the top. Staple the sides and then have the children divide the front of the envelope into three sections, and print at the top of each: giving, praying, fasting. Next have them draw and cut out a dozen or so small flowers (about an inch in diameter) and color them. They should put these flowers in their envelopes.

Spend time discussing some of the items that might fit under each of the three lenten practices, for example:

- Giving…

  …friendship to a lonely person, …one hour of free babysitting, …washing dishes when it's someone else's turn, …folding the family laundry, …picking up litter or recycling.

- Praying…

  …sitting in your prayer corner daily to talk to Jesus, …going to Mass when possible, …receiving the sacrament of reconciliation, …learning and saying new prayers, …saying prayers before and after meals.

- Fasting…

  …giving up one TV program each week, …giving up dessert once a week, …giving up fights with a sister or brother, …giving up some of your time to do a favor for someone.

Invite the children to take the envelopes (with the flowers in them), home to their prayer centers (see Helpful Hint). Every time they do one of the actions on the list above, or any other good deed, they should put a check mark under the proper heading on their envelope and then take out one flower to place near the cross as a decoration.

At the end of Lent, the children will then have a beautiful Easter altar to celebrate the resurrection of Jesus. They might even want to have a family prayer service there. To close this activity, use this beautiful lenten prayer:

God, our Savior / bring us back to you / and fill our minds with your Wisdom. / May we be enriched by our observance of Lent. / Grant this through Jesus Christ, Your Son / who lives and reigns with you and the Holy Spirit / one God, forever and ever. / Amen.

10 More for Lent

Children love boxes, any kind of boxes, so for this lenten activity, capitalize on this by doing a box project that focuses on the poor. I am always surprised at how little children know about what it means to be poor. When questioned, they will invariably describe people who are not rich or people who do not have everything.

Begin by building a "kiosk" (by placing a number of boxes, one on top of the other, with the largest one at the bottom). These boxes can be anchored to one another with tape or glue.

On the front of the structure write the words: "Lent: We Remember Our Poor." Explain to the children that there are various kinds of poverty: not only lack of food, clothing, and shelter, but also lack of education, jobs, love, caring, and support, and lack of faith and of knowledge of God. I encourage children to identify other areas of poverty as well.

Throughout Lent invite the children to bring in pictures of people who are poor from newspapers, magazines, and other sources, and attach the pictures to your kiosk with a thumbtack (not recommended for very young children who might decide to eat the thumbtacks!).

During your lenten prayer times, offer special prayers for brothers and sisters around the world who are poor and for all those who are represented on your kiosk. You might use this or a similar formula: "Dear God, you are our loving Father. Please bless all who are in need today." Then invite the children to pray spontaneously for whomever they wish.

Teacher Info

The activity on this page really helps children become more conscious of the poor and more eager to do something to change situations of poverty. There is an unexpected and welcome carry-over: The children begin to look for and identify the "poor" in their textbooks and in stories that you share. You will need five boxes of various sizes (packing boxes from the grocery store will do very nicely).

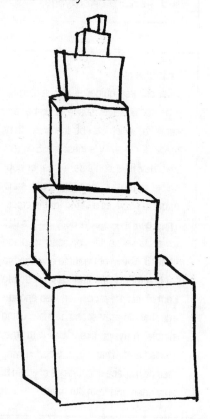

Did You Know?

Lent is closely associated with the transition from winter to spring. The word *lent*, for example, comes from the Anglo-Saxon word for springtime, *lencten*. It describes the gradual lengthening of daylight after the winter solstice.

Already during the 2nd century, Christians prepared for the annual Pascha, or Easter, by fasting for two days. This was a natural thing to do in preparation for the holiest of times when, during the first generations, the Lord's final return was expected. In the 3rd century, this fast was extended to all of Holy Week. A distinct and lengthy season of preparation did not exist until the early 4th century.

Lent evolved around the theme of baptism which, from at least the 3rd century, had been associated with the vigil of the anniversary of the Lord's resurrection: the Easter Vigil. Adults seeking church membership could not just "sign up." They were tested for up to three years. During this day time they were instructed, supported in their withdrawal from pagan practices and loyalties, and taught to live in a new way. Only then were they admitted to candidacy for baptism. Finally, during what would become Lent, they received intense instruction, submitted to exorcisms, participated in special rituals, fasted on Good Friday and Holy Saturday, and were baptized during the Easter Vigil.

—From *Catholic Customs and Traditions* by Greg Dues (Twenty-Third Publications)

MARCH

SUN	MON	TUES	WED	THURS	FRI	SAT

Ideas & Activities

1. Passion Sunday
2. Saints Perpetua and Felicitas
3. Girl Scout Week
4. Plant-A-Flower Day
5. Saint Patrick's Day
6. Saint Joseph's Day
7. Bird Day
8. Liberty Day
9. The Annunciation
10. National Peanut Month

✦ Passion Sunday

Teacher Info

Passion (Palm) Sunday—the Sunday before Easter, and the beginning of Holy Week—reminds us of how tremendously Jesus loves us. He knew that his passion and death would devastate all who would ever love him, so he began that horrible week with a triumphal procession and ended it with the even greater celebration of Easter.

Apparently, this message was well understood in the early church, because Jesus' procession was commemorated year after year in Jerusalem. In the ninth century, Rome adopted the idea of a procession and the blessing of palms for Passion Sunday. Today on Passion Sunday, palms are blessed, a procession is held, and, during Mass, the Passion is read. It is our privilege as catechists to pass on this glorious story to the next generation!

In this activity you will be making your own palms. In preparation for this, tell the children about Passion Sunday, especially how it shows Jesus' great love for us. Or, you might want to read Luke 19:28–40. (In telling or reading the story, I would suggest that you stay with the word "donkey." If you say the word "ass," you'll lose some children completely!)

If possible, begin by showing the children pictures of palms in a religious goods catalog. That way they'll have an idea of what palms are supposed to look like. To make your palms, have available a ruler or a stick for each child. Have children tape strips of green crepe paper onto these.

Now it's time for a procession. As you process—around the room, down the hall, and outdoors if possible—invite the children to sway their palms back and forth as they sing the hymn, "All Glory, Laud and Honor." If your group doesn't sing well, simply have them chant "Hosanna to the Son of God! Blessed is he, who comes in the name of the Lord!"

At the end of your procession, gather back in your prayer space, and call the children to prayer. As the palms sway gently, pray the lovely prayer the church prays before the blessing of the palms. Have the children repeat after you:

God, increase our faith / and listen to our prayers. / Today we honor Christ / our triumphant King / by carrying these palms. / May we honor you every day / by living always in him. / Amen.

This preparation will hopefully make it easier for the children to participate in the liturgy of Passion Sunday in their parishes.

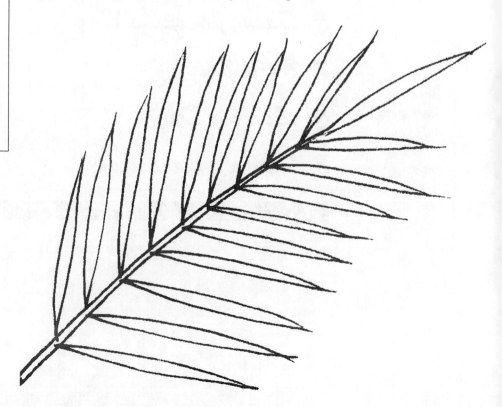

2 Saints Perpetua and Felicitas

Teacher Info

In his book, The History of Black Catholics in the United States, Cyprian Davis, O.S.B., writes, "Two of the greatest martyrs of the early church were two North African women, Perpetua and Felicitas, courageous women whose martyrdom account...occupies an important place in early Christian literature. St. Perpetua was a member of the Carthaginian upper class, and St. Felicitas was a slave, probably of the same household. The martyrdom took place about 203 A.D."

Some African saints, we are told, were black, and some were white, but they had this in common: They loved God intensely! The church celebrates the feast day of Perpetua and Felicitas on March 7.

This activity will give you the opportunity to celebrate God's concept of the races, and to help children develop an appreciation for all God's children.

Begin by holding up one hand, wide open, and declaring that it represents the five races: red, white, black, brown, yellow. Tell the children that God created the various races on earth, and in God's original plan, everyone was supposed to get along. Explain that even though sometimes that doesn't happen, it could, and we can help to make it happen.

Divide your class into three groups (more, if you need them), and tell them to imagine that they are from three different planets, and that so far, the people from these planets have done nothing but fight with one another. Give each group three tasks: name their group and planet, cut out weird creatures to represent the inhabitants of their planets, develop a "peace plan" to make peace with the other planets. (Be sure to limit the time allotted for drawing and cutting out the creatures. While fun, this is not the most important aspect of this activity.)

Suggest that as part of the "peace plan" groups should mention one thing they like about the people of the other planets, one thing they don't like about them, and what they can do to accept the things they don't like.

With some groups, this activity works like magic, with others, the "peace plans" end up starting more wars. If you can get it to work, it is a powerful tool for handling small conflicts–and big ones—by trying to understand the other side, offering solutions, and investing personal effort. If this activity gets off the ground for you, the children will be able to make application to racial conflicts in the future.

At the end of this activity, invite all the "aliens" to come and worship together. Begin by singing, "Make Me a Channel of Your Peace," and then invite children to pray silently for areas in our world where conflict is a way of life. Conclude by praying, "Jesus, our savior and friend, help us to be people of peace, and help us to follow you, as your Saints Perpetua and Felicitas did. Amen."

❸ Girl Scout Week

You might want to begin by telling your class that in the month of March we celebrate Girl Scout Week. Congratulate all the Girl Scouts among you and then introduce the Girl Scout Promise and Law. (If possible, give each child a copy to mount on construction paper and take home and share.) Tell the children that, based on the Girl Scout Promise and Law, you as a class are going to write a "Family" Promise and Law.

On a long piece of newsprint, draw a line at the top and print: "The _____ Family." Explain that the blank will stand for the name of each child's family. Then print: "We will try…" and go point by point through the Girl Scout Promise and Law and apply the principles to family life. Some of the items can be used just as they are, while others need to be adapted. For example: "To live by the Girl Scout Law" can be changed to, "To live by the rules of our family." Promise the children that, at a later date, you will give them copies of this pledge to take home to share with their families.

At the end of this activity, roll up the newsprint reverently, and have a child carry it to the prayer corner. Then have another child hold it up while everyone else points to it, palms up. You (or one of the children) should then pray:

Jesus, Mary, and Joseph, Holy Family, / please bless our families and help our family members / to try to live up to the Family Promises / we have made. / Bless all Girl Scouts and Boy Scouts, / especially those here with us today. / Amen.

Teacher Info

The Girl Scouts and Boy Scouts of the U.S.A. are well known, and in the month of March, we celebrate Girl Scout Week.

As I was doing research for this activity, what caught my attention as a catechist were the Girl Scout Promise and the Girl Scout Law. These are so outstanding that, if they were followed not only by Girl Scouts but by all of us, we could indeed "renew the face of the earth."

The Girl Scout Promise and Law also attest to the fact that, contrary to the notions of some modern national leaders and educators, the basis of our country is Judeo-Christian.

Did You Know?

In case you don't have access to them, here are the Girl Scout Promise and the Girl Scout Law.

Girl Scout Promise
On my honor, I will try
To serve God and my country.
To help people at all times.
And to live by the Girl Scout Law.

Girl Scout Law
I will do my best
To be honest
To be fair
To help where I am needed
To be cheerful
To be friendly and considerate
To be a sister to every Girl Scout
To respect authority
To use resources wisely
To protect and improve the world around me
To show respect for myself and others
     through my words and actions.

4 Plant-A-Flower Day

Teacher Info

When I saw this Plant-A-Flower Day (March 13) on my Country Calendar, I thought, "I just know that there is an activity for religion class here!" And, sure enough, when I thought of a flower, I thought: beauty, fragrance, color, variety, happiness, gardens, home, love, mystery, miracle, Eden, creation, God!

As you can see, this Plant-a-Flower Day not only fits religion class, but if we put our minds to it, we could design a whole scope and sequence chart based solely on the miracle of a flower! If possible, borrow one of those big charts that label the parts of the flower—pistil, stamen, stem, petals, etc.—from a science teacher.

Begin by telling the children about Plant-A-Flower Day. From the chart or from a drawing on the board, show the steps of the development of a real flower. Then tell the children that our actions and the results of them are something like the growth of a flower.

Draw two seeds on the board, one on the right, one on the left. Then invite two children to come forward to help. Have one child stand near each seed. Turn to the child on the right and give a compliment: "You look very nice today!" Under the seed, have the child print, "kind words." Ask the child if the compliment felt good. Then have the child draw a stem, some leaves, and a pretty flower from the good seed. Explain to the children that when we plant a good seed, it grows into something beautiful.

Now, confer briefly with the child on the left, saying in a whisper that what you will say next is make believe. Then, frowning, turn to the child and say: "You look horrible today." Under the second seed, have the child write, "unkind words." Ask the child how your remark felt. Have the child draw an ugly stem, wilting flower, and leaves coming out of this seed. Explain to the children that when you plant a bad seed, something bad comes of it.

Now you and the children can make up a list of "good" seeds that lead to "good" flowers. Here are some examples:

- complimenting someone… makes that person feel good;
- helping someone with math…helps a person succeed in a math test;
- praising parents…helps create a happy family;
- praying… asks for God's blessings;
- smiling at someone…makes a person feel special;
- following Jesus…helps us to reach out to others more often.

Ask the children to decide which of the items on your list they might try to practice more often. Then give them large pieces of paper and ask them to draw a seed growing into a flower. They can label the seed and the flower according to the good action they have chosen.

When all the flowers are finished, carry them to your prayer space and have each child turn his or her resolution into a prayer. For example, a child comes up, shows the drawing, and then prays, "Jesus, please help me to praise my parents more often." After each prayer, all should respond "Amen."

5 Saint Patrick's Day

Teacher Info

St. Patrick, patron saint of Ireland, commemorated on March 17, is so well known that practically any activity we plan will have been done before. So, I came up with the idea of introducing children to other patron saints.

In getting ready for this activity, I noticed that The Catholic Almanac (Our Sunday Visitor, pp. 257-260) lists three pages of patron saints. This is a great resource in so many ways.

In preparation for this activity, you'll need to collect four or five big boxes from the supermarket, different sizes, but all square. (Why not re-use the games from February "More for Lent"!) Make a kiosk out of the boxes by stacking them with the largest one at the bottom. (I usually keep the boxes from sliding by putting several pieces of stick-tack between them.) You can decorate them if you like, but it's not really necessary. Before beginning, you will also need to choose one patron saint (see "Did You Know?" below) for each child. Place these names in a can or box.

Begin this activity by reviewing the lessons for November 1 (about the communion of saints), especially the part that says that the saints in heaven are ready and willing to help us. Then have each child take one of the slips from your can or box.

Next, if you have a Catholic Encyclopedia or a good Lives of the Saints, suggest that the children look up their saints with help as needed. Ask them to print the names of their patron saints and what the saints are patrons of on an 8"x11" piece of paper. They may decorate these if they wish. Give each child a thumb-tack and have them line up around the kiosk and tack their pictures to it. Don't forget to include St. Patrick (perhaps sitting on a shamrock at the top).

Your closing prayer can be held around the kiosk and could begin with "When the Saints Go Marching In." Then have the children pray a litany of saints by naming their patrons, for example, "St. Patrick, patron saint of Ireland…" All can respond, "Pray for us."

Did You Know?
There are patron saints for almost every profession and even for places. Here is a list you can use for the activity above.
St. Matthew—accountants, Bernadine of Siena—advertisers, Francis of Assisi—animals, ecologists, Catherine of Bologna—art, Dominic—astronomers, Sebastian—athletes, Francis de Sales—authors, Vincent Ferrer—builders, Fiacre—cabdrivers, Nicholas of Myra—children, Lawrence and Martha—cooks, Brigid—dairy workers, Appollonia—dentists, George and Isidore—farmers, Flarion—firemen, Ambrose—learning, Jerome—librarians, Gregory the Great and Cecilia—musicians, Camillus de Lellis and John of God, Agatha and Raphael—nurses, Thomas Aquinas and Joseph Colasanz—Catholic schools, Albert—scientists, Benedict—speleologists (care of caves), Clare of Assisi—television.

🌞 Saint Joseph's Day

Teacher Info

St. Joseph is the husband of Mary, protector of the church, patron of workers, and the foster father of Jesus. These are all beautiful and important titles, but what I like best about St. Joseph is that he didn't care that he wasn't always first. In today's world, it is nice to have the example of a saint who was so important, so crucial to God's plan, yet so satisfied to be in the shadows. What a good role model Joseph is for our children, who are so exposed to the philosophy of "me first" and "first place"!

Joseph was both strong and humble. He did more than kings and princes and rulers to move salvation history forward, yet he almost disappears in the telling of its story. The feast of St. Joseph is March 19.

Introduce St. Joseph as a village carpenter in the small town of Nazareth. He was chosen by God to cherish Mary, the mother of Jesus, the Son of God. Joseph was humble, patient, strong, and gentle, giving us a good example of Christian living.

Explain to the children that, though Joseph did many things well that could have made him famous, he didn't feel the need to be first. Then invite the children to role-play incidents in the life of St. Joseph: fleeing into Egypt, sheltering Jesus and Mary, teaching Jesus carpentry.

Next, role-play some situations that occur in children's lives to which they could apply Joseph's virtues: a person winning a skating contest, a person getting the only "A" in the class, a person getting chosen to lead a big city parade. For each scenario, role-play two reactions: 1) humble acceptance and 2) a haughty have-to-be-first attitude.

After the role-play, write on the board, "St. Joseph was…" Then, all over the board—in colored chalk, if you have it—write some of the qualities found in the Litany of St. Joseph: just, chaste, prudent, valiant, obedient, faithful, patient, etc.

Take each quality and invite the children to define it with a "homemade" definition: What does it mean to be just? Then have them apply it to daily life: In what ways can you be just? Go through all the qualities if you have time.

At the end of this activity, gather with the children at your prayer corner and have them pray spontaneous prayers, asking God to be with them and asking for some of the qualities that Joseph had. Conclude with this prayer from the liturgy of the feast of St. Joseph:

Father, with unselfish love / St. Joseph cared for your son / born of the Virgin Mary. / May we also serve you with pure hearts. / We ask this in the name of Jesus the Lord. / Amen.

7 Bird Day

Begin this activity by telling the children that birds can tell us many things about God. Ask them if they think Jesus was a bird watcher. Explain that he obviously watched birds because he speaks about how God feeds them and looks after them. Ask them what this tells them about God. Their response might be that it shows "God cares for the birds…and for us."

Continue to name things that God provides for birds and ask the children to respond with something that God provides for them: God gives birds nice, cozy nests; God gives us homes. God gives birds other birds to be with; God gives us family and friends. God gives birds the ability to sing and chirp; God gives us talents. God gives birds trees and bushes and grass and flowers; God does the same for us.

If possible, and if God has given you a beautiful, crisp, blue-sky day on the day you have this activity, take your class outdoors to observe birds.

As the children enjoy the birds, ask occasionally, "What does that bird tell us about God?" Hopefully, by the time this activity is completed, birds will become tiny "sacramentals," flying about telling children of a loving God.

The ideal closing prayer for today would be to play the song "His Eye Is on the Sparrow," if you can get it on tape or CD. If this isn't possible, then maybe you could just have copies of the words and recite them together. An alternate prayer would be to invite the children to pray a litany of praise to God for the great variety of birds.

Follow this pattern for your litany:

Teacher: We praise you, God, for blue jays…

Children: Thank you, God, for blue jays.

Teacher: We praise you, God, for cardinals…

Children: Thank you, God, for cardinals.

Teacher: We praise you, God, for sparrows:

Children: Thank you, God, for sparrows.

Continue your litany until children have named every bird they can think of.

✵ Liberty Day

Teacher Info

In the United States, liberty (freedom) has a rather lopsided definition. Judging by people's thinking and actions, it seems to mean that we are completely free to do as we like with no restrictions and no obligations toward others. That attitude does not fit into what Jesus teaches us about freedom. He says that, indeed, we are free. How could we not be free and be God's children? But Jesus also speaks in his teaching and parables of how we are to think of others as well as of ourselves.

Therefore, as we exercise God-given freedom in our lives, we have to take a look around us and see how our actions affect our brothers and sisters; we have to consider the common good. How can we as catechists (who may be parents as well) present this to our children, who want to do what they want to do when they want to do it? The only reason I can say confidently that it can be done is that God's own word promises that "nothing is impossible to God." Liberty Day is celebrated March 23.

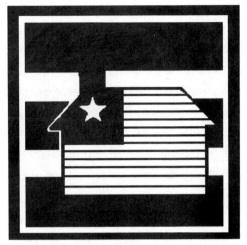

Begin by telling the children that today you will be focusing on liberty and that another word for liberty is freedom. At first, you will see in their eyes that they are thinking red, white, and blue, July 4, and firecrackers, things they usually connect with the words "liberty" and "freedom."

Now, go to the board and print the word "freedom." Under it, and connected to it by lines, print "Rights" on the left and "Obligations" on the right. Under these two, make a big, beautiful heart, and print inside it, "Common Good." Connect the heart to the words "Rights" and "Obligations."

It will probably be necessary to take time to define these terms. Freedom is being able to act, use, move, etc., freely, without constraint. A right is something that is due to us. An obligation is something for which we must take responsibility. Common good is what is best for everyone.

Point to "freedom" on the board and ask: "Are we free to do what we want to do all the time?" If they answer "yes," ask what they would do if they wanted to ride their bike on the sidewalk (or do wheelies), and an elderly person was walking there. Explain we're free most of the time, but there are limits and we need to think of other people.

Now divide your class into small groups and have them make one copy per group of the design on the board. Ask them to think up situations that involve rights and obligations, and then decide what is best for the common good. When children get a good, solid grounding in the art of balancing personal rights and the rights of others, what a lovely world they might build!

End this activity in your prayer corner with the following prayer that uses actions. Form a circle before praying it, and have children repeat it after you:

Jesus, thank you for my rights (both hands point to self) / Please help me, always, to think of others (both hands point outwards) / Help us always to work for the common good (Everyone holds hands, forming a big circle. Then all lift their hands high and sing a resounding "Amen.").

🏵 The Annunciation

Begin this activity with a dramatic reading of Luke 1:26–38, which could be done either by you, a well-coached child, or a parent gifted with outstanding speech skills. (This reading is so full of joy and happiness that a monotonous, second-rate reading of it would be deplorable.) After the reading, pause reverently and then explain that when Mary said "yes" to God, she set in motion the coming of Jesus, our savior, whose life, death, and resurrection opened the doors of heaven for us.

Tell the children that they will be doing a journey-to-heaven activity that shows the value of saying yes to God throughout our lives—as Mary did.

Also cut out a "paper-doll kid" (from an old Sears catalog or a colored ad section from the Sunday paper) and mount it on a piece of cardboard. Place it where the "ME" is. Now point to the "child" on your road and tell the children that this child will be heading toward heaven, by saying yes to God often. Give the children some examples of daily behaviors that give the child opportunities to say yes. For example, God asks the child to do homework well. The child does it. That's a yes. Have a child move the figure a step closer to "heaven."

God asks the child to forgive Danny. The child refuses. That's a no. (No step.) Now have the children think of examples that require a yes or no from them, and have them move the figure accordingly. Little by little, as they follow the step-by-step progress of the child figure, they will get the idea that saying yes to God can happen in many ways every day of our lives. Hopefully this will transfer to more serious matters such as drugs, smoking, stealing, bad companions, and also apply to good things such as courageous and generous Christian social action whenever possible.

If you have time, allow children to take turns getting the child figure from "ME" to "HEAVEN" on the newsprint road, each time they can offer a new example of ways to say yes to God.

To end this activity, call the children to prayer and, since this feast is so joyful, have a procession while playing background music. Again, from my favorite hymnal, *Lead Me, Guide Me*, I suggest either #283, "Here I Am, Lord," by Dan Schutte, S.J., or #284, "Yes, Lord," by Charles H. Hanson. End the procession in your prayer corner by praying the Angelus with your class.

⭐⭐ National Peanut Month

Teacher Info

Peanuts! Peanut butter! What happy events these words conjure up: parties, picnics, school lunches, family activities, treats with friends—many pleasant things.

Did you know that a peanut begins with a little yellow flower that appears at the connection of the leaf to the stem? It appears at sunrise, is fertilized during the morning, and by noon it withers and dies. But at the spot where it has been a little shoot appears, called a peg. That peg grows down toward the ground, pierces the dirt, and keeps growing until it is about 7" long. The peanut seeds are at the end of this peg, and there, underground, the seeds expand and grow into pods and, hurray! we have peanuts!

I decided that there has to be a catechetical treasure hidden in there somewhere, and, sure enough, there is. Let us go then, into the land of the peanut, and find God, our creator, who beckons us to "come and see."

Begin by telling the children about the growth and development of the peanut, and tell them that March has been designated as National Peanut Month. Zero in on the tremendous service given by that little flower, even though its life is short. Explain that just because children are young and have had a short life so far, people think they can't do much to make the world better and bring people to Jesus. Tell them that today you will work together to show what children can do.

Give everyone an 8"x4" piece of paper, and ask them to write something children can do to make the world better (such as shoveling the snow for an elderly or handicapped person), and something children can do to bring others to Jesus (such as praying). You might want to suggest a few other examples with the whole class before they begin writing.

When all are finished, have the children fold the papers and put them into a container. Then go to the board and print at the top of it: "God's Little Peanut Flowers." Have someone pick out the first paper from the container and read it aloud. Have the "author" go and draw a flower on the board and put his or her name beside it with colored chalk. Continue until all are done and you have a whole boardful of God's Little Peanut Flowers.

For the closing prayer, gather everyone in your prayer space and have the children repeat after you:

We are God's Little Peanut Flowers. / We can make this world a better place. / We can lead many others to Jesus. / God, creator, bless us, in Jesus' name. / Amen.

Helpful Hint

When you do special activities that work well and that teach children something important, let others know about it. Send a report about your peanut activity, complete with text and pictures to one of the following: President Jimmy Carter (Plains, Georgia) for use in his Sunday school class; your diocesan office of Religious Education, to let them know that your program is alive and well; and to your local Catholic paper. When you share such activities, you inspire other teachers and catechists to involve children in leading others to God.

APRIL

SUN	MON	TUES	WED	THURS	FRI	SAT

Ideas & Activities

1 April Fools' Day

2 National Garden Week

3 Saint Stanislaus

4 Income Tax Day

5 Saint Marcellinus

6 Saint Mark the Evangelist

7 Saint Catherine of Siena

8 Arbor Day

9 Easter Sunday

10 Easter Octave

April Fools' Day

Begin this activity with a "kill-joy" attitude. Tell the children that today is indeed April Fools' Day, but that in this class there is no time for that nonsense; there is too much work to do. Pass out what looks like a worksheet and ask the children not to turn the paper over until you tell them to do so. Give the directions to take up the pencils, turn the paper over, and write names on the line at the top, as usual.

On the reverse side of the paper, have a line for the child's name and a note that says, "How would you like to sample the new collection of goodies in our class Prize Bucket?" At the strategic moment, call out "April Fools!" and let the children get to your Prize Bucket, which is filled to the top with all kinds of little wrapped candies. (If you have a child with diabetes, be sure to have diabetic sweets among the candies.)

When your relieved and delighted little Christians are chomping away contentedly on the treat, ask how they like this kind of April Fools' joke. Ask them to imagine how they would have felt if you had said that you would give them a treat, but then you had said, "April Fools!" and given them a test instead. Tell them that today they are going to figure out ways to give people happy surprises on April Fools' Day.

You might begin by asking the children to recall any mean things that were done to them on April Fools' Day or mean things they did to others. Challenge children to turn those mean things into happy surprises. For example, a mean thing would be telling someone there is a spider on his or her head. To change this to a happy surprise, you could tell the person about the spider, but, when they brush it off, it's a piece of salt-water taffy!

Discuss as many of these turnarounds as the children can think of and then ask them to write out one way they can give someone a pleasant surprise for April Fools' Day. When all are completed, have children hold these papers up, facing your prayer corner, as you pray:

Jesus, you must have loved surprises / when you were a child. / We love them, too. / Please help us to give / many happy surprises to others / on April Fool's day and always. / Amen.

National Garden Week

Teacher Info

National Garden Week, which is observed on April 10—a good time for growing things—gives us a good opportunity to consider something important: responsibility. People can't grow good gardens unless they are responsible.

Just what is responsibility? The dictionary and the ever-faithful Thesaurus tell us that responsibility means being answerable, being accountable for our behavior, being trustworthy, dependable, reliable, and stable.

The connection between National Garden Week and responsibility then is that both gardening and responsibility come about slowly, with a struggle, and with much care; both result in something very desirable.

Begin this activity by placing your chair so that you have your back to most of the class. Pick up a joke book and begin reading and laughing. Soon, one of the children will ask what you are doing. Answer that you are enjoying your book, and continue ignoring them for another minute or so. The children will no doubt be perplexed by this behavior.

When you turn around, explain that you have just given them an example of irresponsibility. You are the teacher, but you did not take them into account at all. Pick up the book again and read several jokes to the children. Explain that this time you were responsible; you thought not only of yourself, but also of them. Explain that being responsible means people can depend on you. You do what you say you will do and you do it as well as you can. The following guided imagery will help children to understand this in practical terms.

Ask them to close their eyes and imagine that they have been given a small garden patch. Ask them to picture what they would like to grow…which flowers, which vegetables…(pause). Now have them imagine themselves planting the seeds, hoeing weeds, and watering…(pause). Have them picture the plants pushing through the soil, getting bigger and bigger…(pause). Then ask: "What would happen if you decided to walk away from your garden and give up responsibility for it? Picture your garden with no one to care for it. How would it look?"

When the children open their eyes, ask them to describe how they felt about being responsible for a garden. What did they see when they pictured the neglected garden?

Conclude with this prayer:

Dear God, / you make gardens grow, / but you ask us to care for them. / Teach us to be responsible / for all the tasks you give us. (Ask children to pray silently at this point about one particular task for which they need God's help. Pause for a minute or so.) Help us to be / responsible children, students, friends, and gardeners. / We ask this in Jesus' name. / Amen.

🌼3 Saint Stanislaus

Teacher Info

St. Stanislaus is a saint for our times—a saint who was willing to face death in defense of God's law. Stanislaus had wealth, power, and prestige, but he gave it all up to serve God. Because of his courage in denouncing evil and his refusal to play politics, he was killed.

He was born in Poland on July 26, 1030, and, after his early education, he went to Paris for a doctoral degree. After the death of his parents, he gave away his fortune, became a priest, and was appointed Bishop of Cracow in Poland.

The King of Poland, Boleslaus II, was leading a sinful life and giving bad example to the people. Stanislaus confronted him about it, and the king got so angry that he and his guards went to the small chapel where St. Stanislaus was saying Mass. The guards refused to attack this holy man, however, so the king himself murdered him.

The lesson here is to have the courage and fortitude to stand up for what is right. The church observes the feast of St. Stanislaus on April 11.

Introduce Stanislaus to the children and, if you have a map, have them locate Cracow, Poland, on it. Tell them that St. Stanislaus was willing to give up his life rather than keep silent in the face of evil. Explain that the reason he was able to do this was that he had received—as all Christians have—the gift of fortitude.

Explain that fortitude is a gift of the Holy Spirit that we all receive at baptism and that it gives us courage in face of dangers and helps us to put up with hardships for the sake of what is good. Then ask the children if they have ever been in a situation that required fortitude. Discuss this with them.

Next place a chair in the front of the room. Then place a chair on either side of it, both facing the middle chair. Label the chair on the left "Good" and the one on the right "Evil." Ask for three volunteers to sit in these chairs. The one in the center will be the decision-maker.

Now give that child a problem to solve. For example: A friend asks you to go to the mall, but your mother told you to come home right after school. Say to the child, "You have to make a decision. You will need the gift of fortitude."

Then the child sitting in the "Evil" chair should try to influence negatively the decision-maker, while the child in the "Good" chair should use positive influences. The person in the middle then prays to God for help in doing the right thing and makes a decision.

Once the children get the gist of this activity, they will suggest problems they can apply to their lives, and the exchange will become very lively. The children like this activity, because it helps them with situations and decisions that they actually encounter in real life. Explain that it is always good to pray for fortitude, no matter what decisions we have to make.

A good closing prayer might be the opening prayer from the April 11 Mass of St. Stanislaus. Have children repeat the lines after you:

Father, to honor you / St. Stanislaus faced martyrdom with courage. / Keep us strong and loyal / in our faith until death. / Amen.

4 Income Tax Day

Teacher Info

As regularly as the sun and the moon and the stars travel along their appointed orbits comes April 15 and income tax forms.

You might ask why on earth a catechist, who doesn't have to do so, would want an activity for this day! Well, what I have in mind with this activity is less concerned with adults than with children. There are certain things that children can do before and on April 15 to help their parents deal calmly with life situations like tax returns. Children can learn through this activity that their prayers are very important.

Do the best you can to explain Income Tax Day to your little Christians and also explain that their parents (or caregivers) will need love, thoughtfulness, quiet, and prayer as they look over their financial records and prepare their taxes. Tell the children that filing income tax returns is difficult for adults who have to fill out a lot of forms, figure out all kinds of hard things, and often pay additional tax money to the government.

Give each child a sheet of lined paper. At the top, have the children write "Income Tax Day" and under that, "Helper's Sheet." The children can decorate the edges if they like. Explain that there are certain things that children can do on Income Tax Day (and the week or so before) to make that day easier for parents. Suggest a few and write them on the board: be quiet that day, play outdoors instead of indoors, be especially helpful with chores, help care for and entertain younger children, keep the volume down on the TV, and, above all, pray for parents who are working on their income taxes.

Next, ask the children to copy from the board the items that fit their individual families, but be sure to leave spaces on the paper for any additional suggestions parents might want to make.

When the papers are finished, suggest that children take them home and invite their parents to go over them, and then attach the sheet to the refrigerator door (or some other visible place). On or near April 15, you might want to check on the status of the helper sheets and say a prayer together for all those working on income taxes. For your closing prayer, assign children to be readers and give each a copy of this service.

Teacher: Dear God, thank you for our parents and for all the things they do for us.

Reader One: They earn money to pay for our family bills, to buy food and clothing.

Reader Two: They keep our homes running by cooking meals, washing clothes, and cleaning.

Reader Three: Sometimes they have special chores like filing income taxes.

Reader Four: Help them with all these things, dear God.

Teacher: Thank you for our parents and for all your great gifts to us. Amen.

5 Saint Marcellinus

Teacher Info

According to my trusty Lives of the Saints, on April 20 we remember St. Marcellinus, a saint of the early church, who was born in Africa and went into the Alps to spread the gospel. His date of birth is not given, but he died in 374.

Marcellinus worked with all his power for the spread of the kingdom of God. His effectiveness seems to have come from the variety of ways he worked with people: preaching, offering service, prayer, and good example.

Since it is important to begin this activity in an attention-getting way, just walk in, don't say anything, go to the board, and draw a tree with a large trunk, four large branches, and some smaller branches coming out from the larger ones. Label the trunk: "Spreading God's Kingdom." Label the branches: "preaching," "service," "prayer," "good example." Then explain that this big tree is really a symbol of how some saints of the church spread the message about God's kingdom. Tell the class about St. Marcellinus and his mission.

Now invite children to draw leaves on the tree. Begin with the heading "preaching" and explain that it means to tell others about God. Then make a numbered list of ways that children can do this: 1) discuss their religion classes with their family; 2) point out beautiful things and tell of God's goodness; 3) explain to a younger child something about the Mass; or 4) tell or read a bible story to someone. You can make this list as long as you want. Now have a child draw a leaf on the "preaching" branch and put on it the number of one item from the list. If you do it this way, they don't have to try to write out the whole statement. Continue until all the branches are filled with leaves.

"Service" examples can include any kind of service at home, in the neighborhood, at school, at church—all done in God's name, and for the purpose of leading others to God and spreading the kingdom of God.

"Prayer" examples can include going to Mass, saying morning and evening prayers, and inviting others to join them in prayer.

"Good Example" items can include not being ashamed to pray in public or to express faith, helping others, and being cooperative and obedient at home and at school.

To close, gather around the tree and pray the following:

God, our Father / you want all of us to be saved / and come to the knowledge of your truth. / Send workers into your great harvest / that the gospel may be preached / to every creature. / Amen.

6 Saint Mark the Evangelist

Teacher Info

April 25 is the feast of St. Mark, who wrote the second gospel (sometime between the death of Jesus and 60 A.D.). It is believed that he wrote the story of Jesus with the help of St. Peter. This would mean that the story of Jesus that Mark recorded was from an eyewitness, a close follower of Jesus who had been with him from the beginning of his public life until the Ascension. Peter's faith in Jesus was so great that he eventually gave his life for it.

Because Mark recorded his gospel, we are able, centuries and centuries later, still to read about Jesus' words and deeds. If we had to rely only on word of mouth, we would have missed many of the beautiful details.

You could begin this activity by introducing St. Mark, giving as much information as your class can absorb. Then tell the children that sometimes we don't realize how much good we can do by the words we write.

Give each child a 6" x 4" piece of paper and talk about when their written words might do the most good: when sent to a lonely person, an elderly person, a friend, parents, grandparents, their bishop, their mayor, a teacher, a student, the school secretary, a person who doesn't know Jesus, etc. The children can add to this list any persons they want. Have them choose one person from the list and write that name in large letters on their papers.

Then have them tape (or pin) the papers on themselves. Ask a volunteer to come up and read his or her "label" and together discuss what good could be done by writing to this person. If the label says "grandparents," a response might be that a letter makes them happy, helps children keep in touch and learn from grandparents, or keeps grandparents from being lonely.

Then invite the children actually to write to someone before your next class. If they don't know how to address an envelope or write a formal letter, be loving and patient about it, and give them all the help you can.

End this activity by having children write a short note to God on the reverse side of their papers. Encourage them to pray for the gift of preaching that St. Mark had. Have them carry their notes to the prayer area and spend a minute in silent prayer as they talk to God about what they have written.

7 Saint Catherine of Siena

Born in 1347, St. Catherine has been called the most remarkable woman of her time. She would have laughed at the modern notion that women weren't important in the church! St. Catherine was a power for good, and she convinced many people to place their faith in God.

There were problems in Rome at the time, and Pope Gregory XI, who should have been in Rome, was in Avignon, France instead. St. Catherine influenced him to return to Rome and to work for peace there.

Catherine is regarded as one of the finest theologians in the church. She wrote an outstanding work called Dialogue. In 1370, Pope Paul VI proclaimed her a doctor of the church. Besides being a brilliant woman, she was also a peacemaker. In the activity on this page, I would like to focus on her peacemaking abilities. Her feast day is April 29. If possible, have two hand puppets for this activity and pieces of paper.

Share with children what you know about St. Catherine of Siena, highlighting the fact that she was very influential in the church, so much so that she even talked Pope Gregory XI into returning to Rome from Avignon and becoming a peacemaker.

Tell the children that sometimes there are unpleasant situations in families that require peacemaking. Use your hand puppets to demonstrate two siblings fighting over whose turn it is to dust. Ask the children what they could do to make peace in this situation. Encourage them to suggest other situations, for example, arguments over clothing, food, television programs.

When all have had a turn, give the children pieces of paper, 8"x11" or larger, and have them divide the paper into three sections using lines. They should label the bottom section, "The Situation," the middle section, "My Efforts," and the top part, "Peace."

In the bottom section, ask the children to draw one of the conflict situations they have thought of. In the middle section, have them draw a picture of what steps they could take to stop the conflict. In the top section, have them draw a picture of everyone "happy ever after" with peace achieved. When the drawings are finished, invite children to share what they have drawn.

For the closing prayer, clear the middle of the room (or take off for the great outdoors) and form a circle. Have each child come forward to the center of the circle, and hold up his or her drawing, and say, "To my family, the (family name)!" All should respond with this antiphon, "Grant your wonderful peace, dear God! Amen!"

Arbor Day

Teacher Info

From ancient times, people have planted trees in religious ceremonies. In some cultures, trees were planted to celebrate the birth of a child. In the 1800s, people were encouraged to plant trees just to keep the land beautiful. It seems that even in the Garden of Eden (whether real or symbolic), there was an important tree—the Tree of Good and Evil.

Many poems and books have been written about trees. One for children is The Giving Tree, by Shel Silverstein. This little book is about a tree in love, who gave and gave, until there was no more to give. We Christians cannot think of the tree without thinking of the tree of the cross, upon which Love Itself chose to give all there was to give, and more.

Did you Know?

Our modern Arbor Day celebration began with Julius Sterling Morton of Nebraska, who realized that trees were good for the soil and conserved moisture. He suggested that the legislature set aside a day to plant trees. This was done on April 10, 1872. Other states then recognized the value of planting trees and began Arbor Day observances as well. Today many people also observe Earth Day in April. On this day, we are invited to focus on the environment and how we can help our earth to stay healthy. On Earth Day, too, people often plant trees.

If possible, begin this activity with a dramatic reading of *The Giving Tree*. Then let the children talk about how they feel about the tree (and share your feelings with them as well).

Then give the children a long strip of paper, 22"x8" or so. (You can make a paper this size by stapling two 8"x11" pieces together). Have the children divide their papers into four equal sections.

In section one, have them draw a seed, in section two, the shoot of a tree, in section three, a medium-sized tree, in section four, a full-sized tree. Explain that a tree needs a long time to develop and goes through many stages. Trees are created by God and each is unique, just as we are.

Now invite the children to draw one aspect of their own lives in each of the four sections of their papers. In the fourth section they should draw themselves as they think God wants them to be as a fully developed person. Some will see themselves in a profession, others as a mother or father, still others as a good friend or neighbor. When their drawings are completed, invite the children to share what they have drawn.

For your closing prayer, invite children to pray spontaneous prayers of thanks for various kinds of trees and plants and for all the kinds of people there are in the world. You might want to use a litany pattern, for example:

Teacher: For large oak trees that give shade…
All: We thank you, God.
Teacher: For nurses and doctors who help us get well…
All: We thank you, God (and so on).

Easter Sunday

Teacher Info

"This is the day the Lord has made. Let us rejoice and be glad!" (Responsorial Psalm for Easter).

This response sets the tone for Easter. As the Catechism of the Catholic Church (638) says: "The Resurrection of Jesus is the crowning truth of our faith in Christ, a faith believed and lived as the central truth by the first Christian community; handed on as fundamental by Tradition; established by the documents of the New Testament; and preached as an essential part of the Paschal mystery along with the cross: Christ is risen from the dead! Dying, He conquered death; To the dead, He has given life."

Besides the fact that Easter commemorates the Resurrection of Christ from the dead (Mark 16:1–7), two other aspects of the feast cause us to rejoice: Jesus liberates us from our sins; and Jesus opens the way to a new life for us. The activity on this page will touch on these aspects. You can plan to do it anytime before or after Easter.

To begin, show the class a picture of a Paschal candle. (You can either draw one ahead of time, or show a picture of a Paschal candle in a religious goods catalog). Explain that Easter is the most important feast of the church year because Jesus was raised from the dead, and just as he was released from the tomb, we are all released from our sins and given new life! Explain that the big, beautiful candle, which they will see in church at Easter, is called a Paschal candle: a symbol of the Risen Jesus.

Give each child one paper towel roll or one of those long rolls that gift wrapping paper comes on. Have them cover these with white paper (or use spray paint if you dare). At this point, show the children the Paschal candle you have prepared and have them draw the vertical arm of the cross with crayons or felt pens. As they draw this, say together, "Christ yesterday and today…" (as in the Easter Vigil liturgy). Continue with all the symbols, explaining each as you go and praying the appropriate words with each. Then invite the children to decorate their candles as gloriously as possible!

When all are finished, ask them to carry their candles in procession to your prayer space. As they hold them up, invite them to pray three times after you: "Christ is our Light! Thanks be to God!"

Suggest that the children take their candles home to be used as a table decoration on Easter Sunday. Encourage them to lead the table prayer with these words: "Christ is our Light! Thanks be to God!"

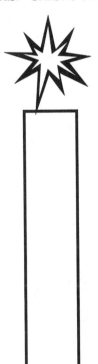

Did You Know?

Here are the other words and symbols used at the Easter Vigil during the "Preparation of the Candle."

"Christ Yesterday and Today" as the vertical arm of the cross is traced.

"The beginning and the end" as the horizontal arm is traced.

"Alpha" as the alpha sign is traced above the cross.

"Omega" as the omega sign is traced below the cross.

"All time belongs to him" as the first number is traced.

"And all the ages" as the second number is traced.

"To him be glory and power" as the third number is traced.

"Through every age forever. Amen" as the fourth number is traced.

☀ Easter Octave

Teacher Info

Easter doesn't end on Easter Sunday, although in our culture it may seem that way. For us Christians, the Monday of Easter is the beginning of the Easter Octave and the celebration goes on.

By definition, an octave is "a period of eight days given over to the celebration of a major feast." Since Easter is the liturgical feast of our year, it is no surprise that our Easter celebration and joy should keep going and going and going! The activity on this page involves making prayer books for the days after Easter. Therefore you will want to do this sometime before the Easter break.

Begin by telling the children what an octave is and then ask them to join you in making Easter Octave prayer books for themselves and their families. Give each child three sheets of 8"x11" paper. Have them put the three sheets together and then fold them. Then give each child a piece of yarn or ribbon to fasten them together, with a bow on the outside of the fold.

On the front page (the cover) have the children print, "My Easter Prayer Book" and decorate it. On the first inside page, have them copy this short prayer: "Holy God, help us to put into action in our lives the baptism we have received with faith" (based on the Opening Prayer of Monday of the Octave of Easter).

On the next page, have them print the Opening Prayer for Tuesday of Easter (notice that I am using only *parts* of these prayers): "Holy God, by this Easter mystery you touch our lives with the healing power of your love." Continue with the Opening Prayer for Wednesday: "Holy God, you give us the joy of recalling the rising of Christ to new life." Thursday: "Holy God, you gather the nations to praise your name." Friday: "Eternal God, you gave us the Easter mystery as a sign of your love and forgiveness." Saturday: "God of love, watch over your chosen family. Give life to all who have been born again in baptism." When all the pages are finished, have the children hold them up as they pray after you:

> Dear Jesus / thank you for the gift of Easter / when we celebrate your new life. / Help us to use these prayers at home / to remember how much you love us / and our families. / Amen.

Be sure the children take their booklets home and encourage them to say one of the prayers each day during the octave of Easter.

MY EASTER PRAYER BOOK

Helpful Hint

Be sure to take time to compliment the children for all their hard work making these booklets. This activity requires more writing than they are probably used to. If your particular class is incapable of this amount of writing, you might want to type the prayers and run them off on a copier. The children can then cut them out and glue them into the little prayer books. But do encourage the children to do the writing themselves—if at all possible.

MAY

SUN	MON	TUES	WED	THURS	FRI	SAT

Ideas & Activities

1. Mother's Day
2. Meteorologist's Day
3. May Altars
4. Litany of Our Lady
5. Our Lady of Light
6. Blessed Josephine Bahkita
7. The Feast of Pentecost
8. Trinity Sunday
9. Memorial Day
10. The Visitation

Mother's Day

You might begin by giving a brief history of Mother's Day and asking the children to share some of the celebrations they've had and the things they've done for Mother's Day. Tell the children that this year you have planned an activity to surprise their mothers (or other caregivers), one that will last all year long. Show the children a commercial coupon book and explain its benefits for getting all kinds of things free or at a reduced price. Then give each child twelve slips of paper, about the size of a coupon in the coupon book. Have them arrange the slips and then you or a helper can staple them into coupon booklets.

On the top of each page, ask the children to print the months of the year, beginning with May and going through to the following April. Ask them to think of things they could do to make their mothers happy. Make a list of these on the board to get them started: cleaning something, doing dishes, babysitting, shoveling snow, setting the table, visiting grandparents. Each page of their booklets should have one promise for making their mothers happy.

When the coupon books are finished, suggest that the children take them home, gift-wrap them, and present them to their mothers on Mother's Day. All year long, Mom can "use" one of the coupons by asking the child-donor to do what is promised.

At the end of the activity, a good closing prayer might be this paraphrase of the Memorare, a prayer to the mother of Jesus. (If possible make a copy for each child.)

Remember, oh most gracious mother Mary, / that never was it known that anyone / who came to you for help / or asked you for guidance / was left without help. / Knowing this, we come to you,/ O Virgin of virgins, our mother. / Loving mother, hear our prayers, / now and forever. / Amen.

Teacher Info

Mother's Day observances began in the United States in 1872, although such observances had been held earlier in England and Yugoslavia. Julia Ward Howe was the first to suggest that there be such a day to honor mothers in the United States, and Mother's Day celebrations were held in Boston. Then Mary Towles Sosseen began a Mother's Day celebration in Kentucky in 1887, and Frank E. Herring started one in South Bend, Indiana, in 1904.

But the celebration that went nationwide was begun by Anna Jarvis of Grafton, West Virginia, on May 10, 1908. In 1915, Mother's Day was made an annual national observance.

Helpful Hint

Some of the children in your class may have lost their mothers either through death or divorce or other reasons. Mother's Day is already painful enough for these children, so try to develop the habit of including not only birth mothers, but any woman who nurtures the child, including aunts, grandmothers, cousins, stepmothers, and neighbors.

2 Meteorologist's Day

Teacher Info

Weather is an important factor in our lives. It affects how we dress, how our food is grown, how we travel, and many other things. Because weather is so important, so are the people who work with weather. Meteorologists have to study many things: the atmosphere, radar maps, satellite photographs, radio waves, and weather balloons to be able to predict weather for us. This is a great service, and truly an important one, and our meteorologists deserve our appreciation.

God created a wonderful and complicated Earth, and gave us the wisdom and skills we need to learn and use its secrets. That's what our meteorologists try to do.

The ideal activity for this day would be to begin with a short prayer in praise of God's beautiful, wonderful creation, our earth, and with a special prayer for all those who serve us as meteorologists. Then invite the children to help you draw up a list of reasons for appreciating our weather forecasters.

Give each child a piece of manila paper. (This kind of paper makes lovely cards because its surface is rather rough and takes crayon well. Avoid felt pens because manila paper is very absorbent.) Ask the children to fold their papers in half, and to draw a line in the center of the cover of the card and print a meteorologist's name there. (Use the names of familiar TV meteorologists.) Direct the children to write the words "Thank You" on the front of the card and then decorate it.

On the inside they should write a note to the meteorologist, wishing them a happy Meteorologist's Day, and saying thanks for service given. Make sure they date and sign their notes. When the cards are finished, collect them, and tell the children that you will be mailing them to the various meteorologists.

A closing prayer for this activity would be to sing God's praises for the various aspects of earth and weather by using this prayer based on Psalm 104.

Side One: We praise your name, Lord our God.

Side Two: You fill our world with so many wondrous things.

Side One: You give us light, the sky, the clouds and rain.

Side Two: You give us storms and lightning.

Side One: You give us oceans, lakes, and streams.

Side Two: You give us mountains, hills, and valleys.

All: We will sing your praises forever, Lord our God. Amen.

❸ May Altars

To make a May altar with your class, you will need a table and a piece of blue or white cloth to cover it—a remnant from a fabric shop will do nicely. Then place boxes of various sizes on the table to form "steps" for flower containers. You will also need rolls of white and blue crepe paper and a few vases or jars.

Cover both the table and the "steps" with the fabric and cut off strips of the white and blue crepe paper (3' to 4' long). Attach these to the wall or bulletin board above the altar with stick-tack or tape, and attach the lower ends to the back edge of your table. Then place a statue of Mary on the "altar."

Here are some possible variations: Fasten pastel-colored silk flowers along the top edge of the crepe paper strips; cut out a seal with a huge "M" on it and attach it to the front of the altar; use candles with paper flames; put gold or silver tinsel here and there for a touch of elegance. Be sure to involve the children in all these preparations, and ask them to bring flowers to class all during May.

Once your May altar is arranged, plan to use this as your prayer space all during May. Have May crownings, Marian-poetry readings, prayer services, and hymn fests there. On your first class in May, gather there to recite the Hail Mary or even say a decade of the rosary together.

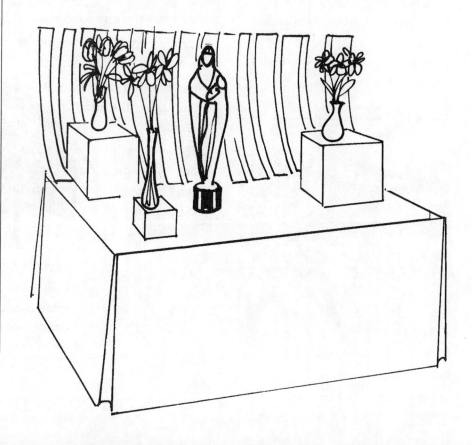

4 Litany of Our Lady

Teacher Info

A litany is a form of prayer that has both a recitation and a response. The Litany of Our Lady uses numerous titles for Mary, and the response is "Pray for Us."

Some of the titles in this litany are: Morning Star, Mirror of Justice, Queen of Peace, Mother of Christ, Mother Most Lovable, Virgin Most Merciful, Virgin Most Faithful, Cause of Our Joy, Mystical Rose, and Queen of All Saints.

The individual titles in the Litany of Our Lady can be used to teach children about virtues and to develop truly beautiful activities for your May classes. Here are a few examples of what I mean:

• Morning Star.

Children can draw a rising sun and a brilliant star off to the side. Discussion can lead to how Mary guides us on the sea of life by her example of prayerfulness, patience, faith, courage, and obedience.

• Mirror of Justice.

The drawing can be an old-fashioned scale with the sides even. The name Mary could be on one side, and the names of troubled areas of the world on the other. Discussion might center around prayers asking for Mary's intercession for the children and their families in these countries.

• Queen of Peace.

The drawing can be a large "M" in the middle of a huge circle with spokes fanning out. Words like countries, homes, churches, families, cities, neighborhoods, individuals, could be at the end of the spokes. Discussion might center on how peace can be achieved in these areas by praying to the Queen of Peace. Attention might also be given to examples of peacefulness in Mary's life.

Begin this activity by choosing from the litany the titles that best fit the children in your class. Have each child choose one title and illustrate it. Under their drawings, have them print the title and the words "Pray for us!" You might have a procession with the drawings to your prayer center while singing a Marian hymn. Then have children attach their pictures to your May altar (or prayer table).

For a closing prayer, have the children form a circle around your "altar" and invite each to call out his or her favorite title of Our Lady. All others respond: "Pray for us!"

Helpful Hint

When you are using an activity that involves a number of titles or choices, occasionally let the children illustrate their choices using clay or play dough. For the activity above, for example, they can illustrate their Marian titles by making simple sculptures with the clay. Don't plan on using this clay again, however, because the children will want to keep their masterpieces.

5 Our Lady of Light

In the beginning of the eighteenth century, a Jesuit priest named Antonio Genovesi from Palermo, Sicily, had a great desire to be a missionary and, in time, he became one. He knew that he couldn't bring people to Christ through his own efforts alone, but that he would need help from heaven. He resolved to carry a picture of Mary to each of his missions and place the people under her protection. However, he was undecided about which picture to take. So he went to consult a "devout lady" who had been receiving apparitions of Our Lady. As the legend goes, Mary appeared to the woman and described how she wanted to be painted, and also that she wished to be called "Most Holy Mother of Light."

For this activity, divide the class into groups and assign them the task of retelling the story of Our Lady of Light or describing what they think she looks like. They can do this through a dramatic re-telling, a skit, a drawing, or any other creative ways they can think of. After this, initiate a discussion on what the message of Our Lady of Light might be for us today (to lighten and brighten the lives of others; to be witnesses of Jesus, light of the world; to spread the light of the gospel in everything we do).

If one of the groups has chosen to draw a picture of Our Lady of Light, have them carry this to your prayer corner. Let each child take a turn holding it up saying, "Our Lady of Light!" to which the rest respond, "Pray for us!" Close by inviting children to pray silently to Mary for light and guidance.

Did You Know?

How did the Our Lady of Light painting get from Palermo, Sicily to Santa Fe, New Mexico? Tradition has it that the original is in the Jesuit church at Leon, Mexico. It is said to have been given to the church by Father Genovesi in 1732. So he must have carried it there as he intended.

In 1898 the history of the picture was translated by Mother Mary Magdalen Hayden. A copy of the picture was given to the Sisters of Loretto by Archbishop Jean Batiste Lamy, first Archbishop of Santa Fe, and stayed in the convent of Our Lady of Light in Santa Fe until recently. The painting is now at Loretto Center in Littleton, Colorado.

—from *Light in Yucca Land* by Sr. Richard Marie Barbour, S.L., Schifani Brothers Printing Company

6 Blessed Josephine Bahkita

Beforehand, prepare a sheet for each child with the four sayings of Mother Josephine Bahkita (see "Did You Know?" below.) Print each saying and follow it with an appropriate question for discussion. To begin this activity, tell the children the story of Josephine Bahkita, highlighting the fact that in spite of great suffering, pain, and misfortune she became a gentle, loving, and holy person. Give each child a copy of the list of sayings and questions and go through all four sayings in a general way. For example, for the first saying, you might ask, How can we know what God wants of us? Point out that this and other questions can sometimes be answered by consulting the bible, by attending liturgy, through prayer, and through other persons. These were very likely ways that Bahkita learned God's will for her.

Once you have gone through the sayings, invite children to close their eyes and reflect on the following statements in silence.

• Blessed Josephine Bahkita was kidnapped and made a slave. If something really difficult ever happened to you, how do you think you would feel? (Pause)

• Josephine eventually had a chance to learn about God and Jesus and Mary which made her very happy. How do you feel about religion? (Pause)

• Josephine believed that we should love everyone as God loves us. How do you feel about this? (Pause)

Close this activity by inviting children to talk to God in silence for a minute or two. Then say the following prayer aloud:

Blessed Josephine, / please ask God to help us to be good, / to love God, / and to pray for those who do not yet know God. / We ask this in the name of Jesus, / our Savior. / Amen.

(NOTE: Although Blessed Josephine Bahkita's feast day is in May, this activity could also be used during Black Heritage Month.)

Did you Know?

Here are some of the sayings of Mother Josephine Bahkita:

•The best thing for us is not what we consider best, but what God wants of us.

•God has loved us so much: We must love everyone...we must be compassionate.

•I can truly say that it was a miracle that I did not die, because the Lord has destined me for greater things.

•Mary protected me even before I knew her.

7 *The Feast of Pentecost*

Teacher Info

The glorious feast of Pentecost occurs fifty days after Easter and is regarded as the birthday of the church. On the first Pentecost, the Holy Spirit came upon the apostles and Mary, as Jesus had promised, and fired them up, making them capable of spreading the good news everywhere.

Since one of the primary faith-learning places for children is the parish church, in the activity on this page we will highlight objects that children see and learn from there.

Make a copy for each child of the following words: altar table, candles, tabernacle, tabernacle light, chalice, votive/vigil lights, the baptistry, holy water, vestments, bells, incense, lectern, lectionary, Stations of the Cross, statues.

Discuss these words and ask if the children are familiar with them. Explain that they are all objects we can find in the parish church. Each in some way reveals something about God. The Holy Spirit, who came to the followers of Christ on Pentecost day, still comes to us today. One way is through our liturgy and the sacred objects we use at church. Ask volunteers to explain each object. Then assign each child one of the objects and have him or her draw a picture of it (with assistance from you, where needed). When all the drawings are complete, process with them to your prayer space for this closing prayer ritual.

Have each child take a turn holding up what they have drawn, while saying: "Come Holy Spirit, teach us through the altar table," or "Come Holy Spirit, teach us through the lectionary." All should respond: "Come, Holy Spirit, Come."

Encourage children to share their word lists and drawings with parents at home and to try to identify each object the next time they go to church.

Did You Know?

There are many traditional prayers addressed to the Holy Spirit. The following is one of the most popular.

Come Holy Spirit, fill the hearts of
Your faithful and kindle in them
The fire of your love. Send forth
Your spirit and they shall be created,
And you will renew the face of the earth.

8 Trinity Sunday

Teacher Info

When I reflect on the mystery of the Holy Trinity, I'm always glad to have St. Patrick on one side of me and St. Augustine on the other. I like St. Patrick's idea of the three leaves on one shamrock, and I enjoy St. Augustine's analogy that trying to understand mystery is like attempting to get the ocean into a little hole on the shore. The simplicity of these gives me confidence.

Trinity Sunday is the Sunday after Pentecost, and it celebrates "the most sublime mystery of our faith." There are Three Divine Persons in one God (Mt 28:18–20). What better way is there to bring the mystery of the Holy Trinity down to earth than by using the glorious sign of the cross?

Share with children St. Patrick's symbol for the Blessed Trinity and also St. Augustine's analogy. Explain that another symbol of the Trinity is the sign of the cross. Go to the board and draw a large cross. Next to it, write: "God the Father created us. God the Son redeemed us. God the Holy Spirit makes us holy."

Have the children look and listen as you make an "explaining" sign of the cross: "In the name of the Father, who created me, and of the Son, who redeemed me, and of the Holy Spirit, who makes me holy." Suggest that the children take turns standing up and making the sign of the cross in such a way that it shows how proud they are to be followers of Jesus and that they believe in the Holy Trinity.

Then pass out small pieces of paper and ask the children to fold them in half and make and decorate a cross on the front. Inside the paper, have them write the words, "In the name of the Father, and of the Son, and of the Holy Spirit. Amen."

Then, on the inside of the cover, have them write these "code" words that remind them what making the sign of the cross means: Belief, Trinity, Christianity, Pride. Explain each of these as follows.

- Belief: I believe in the Holy Trinity: Father, Son, and Holy Spirit.
- Trinity: I witness to God the Father as creator; God the son as redeemer; and God the Holy Spirit who makes us holy.
- Christianity: I am a follower of Jesus Christ who loved us so much that he died on the cross for us.
- Pride: I am proud to be a Christian, a believer, a follower of Jesus.

For your closing prayer, begin with the sign of the cross, and then pray the Glory Be together:

Glory be to the Father / and to the Son / and to the Holy Spirit, / as it was in the beginning, / is now, / and ever shall be, / world without end. / Amen. (Conclude with the sign of the cross.)

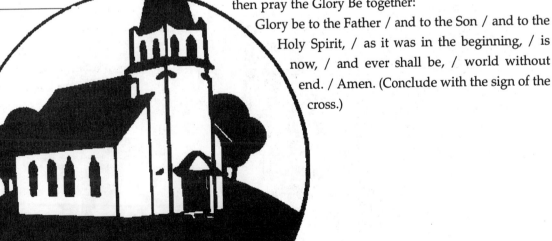

Memorial Day

Usually around Memorial Day nature is beautiful, full of flowers, green grass, and all sorts of lovely things. We are going to capitalize on that in this activity.

Give each child a piece of 8"x11" paper, preferably manila paper, if you have it. Have them draw a large wreath, almost filling the paper. Then they can either cut out pictures of flowers and glue them on the wreath or draw the flowers directly on the wreath and color them in.

Have the children cut out these wreaths, make a little hole at the top, and slip a piece of yarn or ribbon in it to serve as a hanger. Explain that it is a Memorial Day custom to place wreaths on the graves of people who have died in wars. Wreaths are also placed on graves of friends and relatives on special occasions throughout the year.

Now ask children to stand and hold their wreaths as you lead them in the following prayer:

Jesus, we ask you to bless all those who have died, in particular _____ (pause). / We ask you to bless, too / all those who have died in wars (pause). / With these wreaths we pay them tribute. / Let them remind us to pray often / for those who have died. / Amen.

Suggest that the children take the wreaths home, hang them up in a place of honor, and invite family members to join them in praying for the dead.

1·0 The Visitation

Begin with a dramatic reading of Luke 1:39–56. (I say "dramatic" because it's a glorious and passionate story, and must be presented as such or its power is diminished.) If you have time, break the reading into parts and allow the children to read it with you.

After the reading, spend time talking about it. What did the children learn from it? Suggest that one lesson is that both Mary and Elizabeth expressed great joy in God's plan for them.

On the board (or on a large poster) write, "My spirit finds JOY in God, my Savior" (Luke 1:47). Tell the children that this is one of the lines from the reading about the Visitation, and have them say it aloud at least five times, each time more fervently.

Next, give each child a piece of brightly colored paper and have them cut out several large "gems" (shapes of any kind) to paste on the JOY letters. Each time they paste one on, they should think of something that gives them joy and say silently, "Thank you, God, for_____."

When the letters are covered with gems, have the children put strings on them for hanging and then tape them around or near your prayer space. Then gather there and sing "I've Got that Joy, Joy, Joy, Joy, Down in My Heart."

There is so much sadness in our world, our homes, and our neighborhoods these days that it's good if we can help our young Christians find and express joy in God their savior!

Teacher Info

The Feast of the Visitation (May 31) celebrates life—Elizabeth carries John, the Precursor of Jesus, in her womb, and Mary carries Jesus, the Son of God. This Feast of the Visitation has so much Christian beauty in it that it was difficult to decide upon an activity. However, since joy was a possibility, I settled on that.

There are many other possible themes: forgetting oneself to serve others, singing songs of praise, believing in God's power and care, and recognizing one another's gifts and graces.

For this activity you will need string, tape, and huge cut-out letters that spell "JOY." Make them at least a foot long and deep enough to have decorations glued to them. If possible, have more than one set of letters. Also have copies of the Magnificat (as below) for children to use as a closing prayer.

Did You Know?

When Mary greeted Elizabeth, she broke into a glorious song of praise called the Magnificat. Here is a shortened and paraphrased version of it for children.

I praise you God with all my heart,
and I rejoice because you are my savior.
You care for me so much that from now on
all people will call me blessed.
You have done great things for me,
and holy is your name…
I praise you God with all my heart. Amen.

JUNE

SUN	MON	TUES	WED	THURS	FRI	SAT

Ideas & Activities

1. Teacher Appreciation Week

2. National Yo-Yo Day

3. Children's Day

4. The Feast of Corpus Christi

5. Prayers Before and After Meals

6. Saint Charles Lwanga and Companions

7. Saint Barnabas

8. Four Ways To Pray

9. Summer Project for Jesus

10. Closing Up Shop for the Year

Teacher Appreciation

Begin by telling the children that this is Teacher Appreciation Week and that you have a question about it. Ask, "Who teaches?" They will no doubt respond that teachers teach. Explain that while this is correct, it is not necessary to teach in a classroom in order to be a teacher. Ask the children if someone (a parent or grandparent, for example) has ever taught them a skill. Tell them that although this person is not a classroom teacher, they are still a teacher. They might understand this better if you give them a little formula to use. For example, "I know how to (skill). I learned it from (person's name). Therefore, (person's name) is a teacher." Have them take turns using the formula, naming someone who has taught them a particular skill or idea or fact.

When you have gotten the idea across, give the children pieces of paper and invite them to make thank-you cards, one for their classroom teacher and one for someone who is a teacher, but not in the classroom.

Close with the following prayer ritual:

Teacher: During Teacher Appreciation Week, good and gracious God, we thank you for having taught us the best lesson of all: that you love us.

Children: Thank you, God, for loving us.

Teacher: Many people in our lives have taught us valuable lessons, especially our parents…

Children: Thank you, God, for our parents.

Teacher: Our teachers in school and in religion class have taught us about God's great love for us…

Children: Thank you, God, for our teachers and catechists.

Conclude by inviting children to pray aloud for classroom and other teachers who have taught them valuable lessons.

2 National Yo-Yo Day

Teacher Info

My calendar says that on June 6 we celebrate National Yo-Yo Day. I like yo-yos. In fact, I love yo-yos! They have baffled me, challenged me, at times conquered me, and helped develop in me the ability to struggle with something until I achieve my goal.

It is for all these reasons that I looked for a way to connect yo-yos with an activity for religion class. It didn't take me long to find it. In the yo-yo are lessons in perseverance, patience, and determination, and aren't those the very qualities needed to develop virtues? Yo-yos and virtues. We know what a yo-yo is. As for virtue, here is a simple definition: A virtue is a habit of goodness, acquired by repeated good actions.

Did You Know?

The church has always placed emphasis on the value of growing in virtue. The three greatest virtues are faith, hope, and charity. Others are prudence, temperance, justice, patience, humility, joy, peace, goodness, modesty, and self-control. The seven Gifts of the Holy Spirit are also virtues and they are wisdom, understanding, knowledge, fortitude, counsel, piety, and fear of the Lord.

If you have a way of attracting minor miracles, it is conceivable that you might have enough yo-yos for each child in your class. But, if not, a few will do. Have the children work the yo-yos. (If some children don't know how to use a yo-yo, just pair them with some of the experts.)

When they have played with them for a while, ask the class what was needed to succeed in working the yo-yo. Lead them to staying with the job, being willing to start over again and again, having patience, having determination, practicing. Next, ask the children what is needed to overcome a bad habit like lying or disobeying parents or not doing their homework on time. Could they use these same requirements? Yes, and they should also add prayer to the list.

Now, give the children pieces of paper and ask them to draw a large yo-yo. Inside the yo-yo, have them print something they would like to learn to do and something they would like to learn to be. Around the yo-yo have them print the requirements that fit. (If some child decides to be president of the United States and wants to know if he or she should write "pray," my response would be, "Of course!")

When all the drawings are finished, have the children take turns sharing them with the rest of the class. When all have had a turn, have the children carry them in procession to your prayer area. As they hold them high, you (or a child) can lead them in this closing prayer.

Jesus, our special friend / please help us to do and to be / the things that are on our posters / and to keep trying for love of you. / We ask this in the name of the Father / and of the Son / and of the Holy Spirit. / Amen.

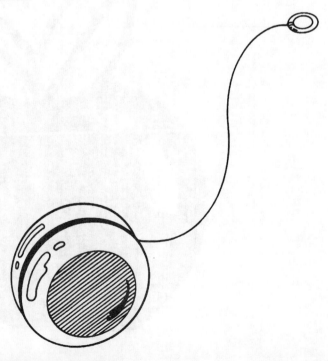

3 Children's Day

To begin, divide your class into groups of four to six children, fewer if possible. Tell them that this is Children's Day and that you are going to give them a chance to take one story about Jesus and present it their way.

Put these general group guidelines on the board: 1) choose your story about Jesus; 2) decide how you will present it to the rest of us; 3) tell us what the story teaches through your presentation. Designate a definite time limit, so the groups know exactly how much time they have. Suggest that they might present their stories through skits, drawings, dramatic readings, pantomime, song, interviews, or in any other ways they can think up.

Then, step out of the way and let what happens happen—and only God knows what will happen! (With this kind of activity, my biggest problem has always been staying out of it and not imposing my way of doing things.) Do walk around as they work, however, and if they ask for your input you can give it. Your close presence will also help to keep order.

When all the presentations have been made, you might want to gather in a circle and make little speeches of appreciation to individuals and groups, making sure that no one gets left out. The closing prayer should be the children's choice—of course!

It is quite possible that you will learn through this activity some new ways to engage your class in bible study. One thing is for sure: If you handle "freedom" gently on Children's Day, the children will go home happy, loving Jesus, and loving you (and they'll be more ready for the more structured classes ahead).

4 The Feast of Corpus Christi

Teacher Info

Corpus Christi is celebrated on the Sunday after Trinity Sunday. It is a day that is set aside by the church for us to focus on the belief that Jesus is present in the eucharist (Matthew 26:26–28). The feast has been celebrated in the church since 1264.

As with many great mysteries of faith, it isn't easy to bring what we adults know and feel to a child's level. However, children can understand that Jesus is with them and that the eucharist is a very particular sign of his presence. He is truly present in the bread and wine because he loves us and wants to be with us.

For details about the church's teaching on the eucharist, see the Catechism of the Catholic Church (1322-1419).

Begin this activity by standing in front of the room, placing your hand over your heart, and telling children that you love each and every one of them, and even though they can't see your love, it's there.

Then, if available, show a picture of a host and chalice. Tell the children  that at Mass the celebrant repeats the words of Jesus over the bread (host), "This is my Body" and over the wine (chalice), "This is my Blood." Jesus first said these words to his followers at the Last Supper the night before he died on the cross. He concluded by saying, "Do this in memory of me."

Explain that, like your love for them, which is present but can't be seen, Jesus is in the bread and wine, even though we don't see him. Explain, too, that this is a mystery of faith, not something we can understand with our limited ways of thinking. We believe it because Jesus said it, and we believe Jesus!

At this point, if possible, take the children to your parish church and give them time to pray before the tabernacle. At the end of this prayer time, explain that Jesus is also with us in God's word in the bible and through the Holy Spirit. In all three ways, the important thing is to remember that Jesus is with us always. When we celebrate Eucharist, read the bible, and pray to the Holy Spirit, we do it in memory of Jesus.

Pray the following closing prayer together (either in church or in your prayer corner).

Teacher: Jesus, help us to remember that you are always with us. Believing that you are present, we offer you our needs and concerns.

Reader One: For all our brothers and sisters around the world, that we may live in peace and harmony, let us pray to the Lord…

All: Lord Jesus, hear our prayer.

Reader Two: For all our families and friends, near and far, that God will watch over them and bless them, let us pray to the Lord…

All: Lord Jesus, hear our prayer.

Reader Three: For all those in our parish family who are preparing to receive communion for the first time, let us pray to the Lord…

All: Lord Jesus, hear our prayer.

Teacher: Jesus, thank you for hearing our prayers. May we remember that you are with us always. Amen.

5 Prayers Before and After Meals

Teacher Info

In our fast-moving culture, families don't get together for meals as often as they used to. When they do get together, it would be great for the children in our classes to be prepared to pray a Blessing Before Meals and Grace After Meals. The activity on this page will focus on this.

If at all possible, have available a large cookie for each child, as well as napkins and pieces of lined paper.

Did You Know?

Here are the formal meal prayers that many Catholics still pray before and after meals.

Blessing Before Meals: "Bless us, O Lord, and these your gifts, which we are about to receive from your bounty, through Christ Our Lord. Amen."

Grace After Meals: "We give you thanks for all your benefits, Almighty God, who lives and reigns forever. May the souls of the faithful departed, through the mercy of God, rest in peace. Amen."

Begin this activity by forming a large circle and passing out a napkin and a cookie to each child. Remembering that you are dealing with children, and that the spicy aroma of your cookies might be blocking out everything else, ask them to hold their cookies patiently until grace has been said. Then say a short blessing before you eat. When every last crumb has vanished, say a prayer after eating.

Now, give the children a piece of lined paper and ask them to write their own brief before-meal prayers. After a reasonable time, let those who wish share them. Pronounce all the prayers good, because children's prayers are always good. Then ask for volunteers to role-play a family sitting down to eat, with some members beginning to eat before the meal prayer has been said. One of the "parents" should explain how important it is to thank God, and then pray a spontaneous blessing before meals. Direct the players, as needed, encouraging them to be reverent and prayerful.

With different children role-playing, use a similar procedure for grace after meals. Perhaps in this case, one of the children jumps up to leave the table before the grace has been said. The parent should explain the importance of thanking God after a meal, and then pray a spontaneous prayer of thanks.

When the role-playing is over, ask the children to write a grace after meals beneath the prayer before meals. They can decorate their papers and take them home for use at family meals. Before you close, tell the children about the formal prayers that Catholics always used in the past for meal prayers.

As your closing prayer, say both prayers (see "Did You Know?" left) line by line and have the children repeat them after you.

6 Saint Charles Lwanga and Companions

Begin this activity by telling the story of St. Charles Lwanga and his companions, accenting their youth and courage and the great love they had for Jesus for whom they gave their lives. Ask: "What are you willing to give up in order to serve Jesus better and show your love for him?" After discussing this question (and explaining that when we occasionally say no to ourselves, we are strengthening our characters), give out strips of paper and ask the children to print one or two things they are willing to give up for love of Jesus, thus becoming stronger Christians. Make some suggestions: no television for a day, computer games, snacks, etc. The strips should not be signed. Collect them or have a helper do it; then have children take turns reading the messages on them aloud. Invite discussion.

When all the strips have been read and discussed, remind the children that St. Charles and his companions not only gave up things for love of Jesus, but gave up their very lives. Tell them that Jesus does not ask us to give up our lives, but he does want us to learn to give up smaller things so that we can be strong Christians when hard decisions come up.

Now move to your class prayer corner and have the children place the strips in a basket. Ask them to close their eyes and speak to Jesus about one thing they are willing to give up for love of him. Remind them to ask Jesus for his help in what they have decided to do.

This activity could end with the very appropriate hymn, "I Have Decided to Follow Jesus, No Turning Back!"

7 *Saint Barnabas*

St. Barnabas was not one of the original twelve apostles. I like him for that very reason. He says to me that you don't really have to be at the top or first in line to do a good job in God's kingdom.

Besides, Barnabas was wonderfully "human." He befriended St. Paul and had a great deal to do with Paul's becoming the Apostle of the Gentiles. However, when Paul wouldn't take John Mark, Barnabas' young nephew, on their second missionary trip, Barnabas put his nose in the air, and stomped off to Cyprus with John Mark, leaving Paul in Antioch! (Acts 15:30–40).

The children will love Barnabas. At first they might question his right to be a saint. Our job as catechists is to lead them to the realization that we can't judge who is or is not a saintly person. Also someone who appears to be a great sinner, might someday deeply repent.

As soon as class begins, tell the children that you are leaving and walk toward the door. Hesitate at the door and then turn back and ask the children why they think you are going out before class has gotten under way. Listen to their guesses and then explain that nobody can really know, except God and you. Tell them that, in fact, you weren't really going to leave at all. Explain that most of the time we can't really know why people do what they do. That's why Jesus asks us not to judge!

Now tell them about St. Paul and Barnabas. Have children take turns reading the account in Acts 15:30–40, and perhaps role-play it afterward. Explain that it would be easy to judge Barnabas and say that he would never be a saint, but God could see what was in Barnabas' heart—and Barnabas is indeed a saint.

Now give the children a piece of paper and have them fold it in half. Ask them to remember a time when they saw someone doing something and judged wrongly about what they saw. On one side of the paper, ask the children to draw what they saw and under that drawing to write, "I thought that…" and complete the sentence. On the other side of the paper, have them draw the identical drawing. Under that one, they can write, "But, this is what really happened…" (Example: I thought that Moe was stealing Mrs. Manning's apples…. But, this is what really happened: Mrs. Manning was not well and asked Moe to pick the apples for her.)

After the papers are finished, share their responses. Then process to the prayer corner singing: "Whatsoever you do…" Once there, invite the children to pray silently about times they may have misjudged others. Then pray aloud, with the children repeating after you:

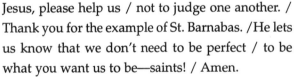

> Jesus, please help us / not to judge one another. / Thank you for the example of St. Barnabas. /He lets us know that we don't need to be perfect / to be what you want us to be—saints! / Amen.

✸ Four Ways To Pray

Begin by asking, "What is prayer?" (Prayer is the lifting up of our minds and hearts to God.) Write the word "Prayer" on the board, and explain that there are different reasons why we pray. To illustrate this, under the word prayer, write: "We pray to adore God, to thank God, to tell God we're sorry, and to ask God for what we need." Then ask the children: "Where and when can we pray?" (Anywhere! Anytime!)

Give out large pieces of poster paper, and tell the children that they will be making reminder posters for themselves (to help them remember to pray during the summer). At the top have them print, "Remember to Pray," and under that in large letters "1) Adore, 2) Thank, 3) I'm Sorry, 4) Ask." Allow time for decorating these posters. Suggest that they place them in their rooms at home and every time they say a prayer, place a check somewhere on the poster. (Maybe by the end of summer their posters will be covered with checks!)

Now talk about when and where to pray. Explain that even though it's true that we can pray anywhere and at all times, it helps to have a simple plan for ourselves. Ask for some examples of where and when children can pray during the summer: Mass (Sunday and some weekdays), their rooms (upon awakening and before going to bed), in the dining room (meal time and anytime), and outdoors (anytime).

Conclude this activity by inviting the children to your prayer space and praying an example of all four types of prayer. Encourage spontaneous responses. You can begin each set by offering examples like these:

Adore: Oh God, you are more wonderful than I can say.

Thank: Thank you, God, for the wonderful children in my class.

I'm Sorry: Forgive me, loving God, when I make mistakes.

Ask: Please bless our world with peace, great God.

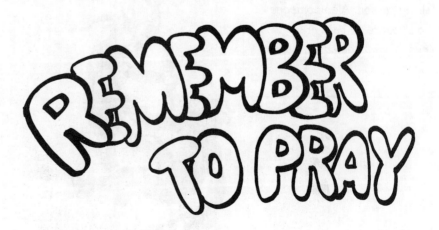

Summer Project for Jesus

Teacher Info

When I was teaching at St. Jude School in Montgomery, Alabama, we did something one year that was lot of work, but was a tremendous help for families. We prepared Summer Activities Booklets for levels Primary (K-3), Intermediate (4-6), and Junior High (7-8). Each teacher drew up a list of possible activities for his or her grade and sent it to the collator—me! When I got the lists, I edited, typed, and added a little artwork. It wasn't a masterpiece, but the idea was great and there was enough material in the booklets to solicit deep gratitude from our families.

Begin by giving the children pieces of cardboard and ask them to draw and cut out a vehicle—it doesn't matter what kind. It can be a bus, snowmobile, bike, car, van, dune-buggy, or motorcycle. Then give them long, narrow pieces of paper, 8"x22" or so, and ask them to draw a road with as many houses along it as they have family members—don't forget grandparents!

When the houses are in place, have the children put names or initials of family members on each house. Then explain that during the summer, every time they do something to make a family member happy or help to bring them closer to Jesus, they should put a star on that house. Suggest that if they want to keep a record of what they have done, they can write the good deed in "code," on their vehicle and keep it in a secret place. (The "code/secret" angle is attractive to children.) When the project is finished, have the children fold the vehicle inside their papers and take them home.

For your closing prayer offer the children this summer blessing (borrowed from *Religion Teacher's Journal*), with your right hand extended in their direction:

> May God, Father, Son, and Holy Spirit,
> watch over you and keep alive in your heart
> the faith-teachings you have learned this year.
> Keep your mind and heart on God.
> Remember to pray often and to celebrate your faith
> at home and at Mass with your family.
> May the God of creation, the God who comes to us in Jesus,
> the God who dwells with us in the Holy Spirit,
> keep you safe, happy, and holy this summer. Amen.

✦ Closing Up Shop

Teacher Info

Here is a simple form letter you can use to keep in touch with the children in your class.

Dear (child's name),

Thank you for all you did this year to make our religion class pleasant and wonderful. Your greatest contribution to our class has been (name it). You have been a fine member of this class and a big help to me.

If you have any questions or things you need help with during the summer, you can contact me at: (give address and phone). Even if you don't have questions, I will be glad to hear from you.

Let's continue to pray for one another and for all the members of our class.

Love,

(Your name)

Once classes are over, don't lose touch with the precious little ones you have been teaching. Keep in touch by writing each child a letter to be read and re-read over the summer. A week or two after classes are over, mail them to the children's homes. If you don't have time for personal letters, prepare a simple form letter, something like the one under "Teacher Info." You can decorate the letters if you have time, and perhaps enclose a prayer card. Of course, a personalized letter is the best of all.

You will notice that the form letter assumes that the children have been a pleasure to be with. When it comes to one or two children in your group you will no doubt hesitate to say that they gave you joy. But do try to come up with some contribution they made to the class, no matter how small.

In my teaching days, I would get ideas for my letters from the children themselves during our last class of the year. While enjoying refreshments, we would sit around in a circle to share the best and worst moments of the year. (Don't be surprised if their "best and worst moments" aren't the same as yours.) I would also ask them to share what they thought they had contributed to the class. This generated a lot of information and enabled me to personalize the letters as much as possible.

A Blessing for Catechists
May God bless and reward you
for sharing your time and talent with God's little ones.
May you grow in faith, love, hope, and joy this summer,
and may you be renewed and refreshed
by this time away from teaching
so that your zeal and enthusiasm
will have you looking forward to another year
of proclaiming God's word with all your heart. Amen.

Of Related Interest...

Celebrating Holidays
20 Classroom Activities and Prayer Services
Stacy Schumacher and Jim Fanning
The authors give a decidedly spiritual dimension to traditional secular holidays such as Columbus Day, President's Day, Labor Day, Earth Day, April Fool's and others.
ISBN: 0-89622-611-5, 136 pp, $12.95

Learning by Doing
150 Activities to Enrich Religion Classes for Young Children
Carole MacClennan
A systematic yet simple lesson wheel approach where the topic is reinforced through sensory activities designed to engage the attention of young children.
ISBN: 0-89622-562-3, 136 pp, $14.95

When Jesus Was Young
Carole MacClennan
This book helps children in grades K-5 understand the life and times of Jesus through activities such as grinding wheat for bread and weaving a mat.
ISBN: 0-89622-485-6, 80 pp, $7.95

Leading Students Into Prayer
Ideas and Suggestions from A to Z
Kathleen Glavich
The author explores the varied forms that prayer takes—personal and communal, vocal and mental, liturgical, Scripture-based, centering, and traditional.
ISBN: 0-89622-549-6, 160 pp, $12.95

Available at religious bookstores or from
TWENTY-THIRD PUBLICATIONS
P.O. Box 180 • Mystic, CT 06355
1-800-321-0411